# CASANOVA'S HOMECOMING

## LECTOR HOUSE PUBLIC DOMAIN WORKS

# CASANOVA'S HOMECOMING

ARTHUR SCHNITZLER,
EDEN PAUL,
CEDAR PAUL

9 789356 146426
ISBN: 978-93-5614-642-6

Published: 1922



LECTOR HOUSE

LECTOR HOUSE LLP
E-MAIL: info@lectorhouse.com

# CASANOVA'S HOMECOMING

BY

ARTHUR SCHNITZLER

TRANSLATED BY
EDEN AND CEDAR PAUL

1922

# CONTENTS

# CHAPTER I.

Casanova was in his fifty-third year. Though no longer driven by the lust of adventure that had spurred him in his youth, he was still hunted athwart the world, hunted now by a restlessness due to the approach of old age. His yearning for Venice, the city of his birth, grew so intense that, like a wounded bird slowly circling downwards in its death flight, he began to move in ever-narrowing circles. Again and again, during the last ten years of his exile, he had implored the Supreme Council for leave to return home. Erstwhile, in the drafting of these petitions—a work in which he was a past master—a defiant, wilful spirit seemed to have guided his pen; at times even he appeared to take a grim delight in his frowardness. But of late his requests had been couched in humble, beseeching words which displayed, ever more plainly, the ache of homesickness and genuine repentance.

The sins of his earlier years (the most unpardonable to the Venetian councillors was his free-thinking, not his dissoluteness, or quarrelsomeness, or rather sportive knavery) were by degrees passing into oblivion, and so Casanova had a certain amount of confidence that he would receive a hearing. The history of his marvellous escape from The Leads of Venice, which he had recounted on innumerable occasions at the courts of princes, in the palaces of nobles, at the supper tables of burghers, and in houses of ill fame, was beginning to make people forget any disrepute which had attached to his name. Moreover, in letters to Mantua, where he had been staying for two months, persons of influence had conveyed hope to the adventurer, whose inward and outward lustre were gradually beginning to fade, that ere long there would come a favorable turn in his fortunes.

Since his means were now extremely slender, Casanova had decided to await the expected pardon in the modest but respectable inn where he had stayed in happier years. To make only passing mention of less spiritual amusements, with which he could not wholly dispense—he spent most of his time in writing a polemic against the slanderer Voltaire, hoping that the publication of this document would serve, upon his return to Venice, to give him unchallenged position and prestige in the eyes of all well-disposed citizens.

One morning he went out for a walk beyond the town limits to excogitate the final touches for some sentences that were to annihilate the infidel Frenchman. Suddenly he fell prey to a disquiet that almost amounted to physical distress. He turned over in his mind the life he had been leading for the last three months. It had grown wearisomely familiar—the morning walks into the country, the evenings spent in gambling for petty stakes with the reputed Baron Perotti and the latter's pock-marked mistress. He thought of the affection lavished upon himself by his hostess, a woman ardent but no longer young. He thought of how he had passed his time over the writings of Voltaire and over the composition of an audacious rejoinder which until that moment had seemed to him by no means inadequate. Yet now, in the dulcet atmosphere of a morning in late summer, all these things appeared stupid and repulsive.

Muttering a curse without really knowing upon whose head he wished it to alight, gripping the hilt of his sword, darting angry glances in all directions as if invisible scornful eyes were watching him in the surrounding solitude, he turned on his heel and retraced his steps back to the town, determined to make arrangements that very hour for immediate departure. He felt convinced that a more genial mood would possess him were he to diminish even by a few miles the distance that separated him from the home for which he longed. It was necessary to hasten, so that he might be sure of booking a place in the diligence. It was to leave at eventide by the eastward road. There was little else to do, for he really need not bother to pay a farewell visit to Baron Perotti. Half an hour would suffice for the packing of all his possessions. He thought of the two suits, the shabbier of which he was wearing at that moment; of the much darned, though once elegant, underlinen. With two or three snuffboxes, a gold watch and chain, and a few books, these comprised his whole worldly wealth. He called to mind past splendors, when he had travelled as a man of distinction, driving in a fine carriage; when he had been well furnished both with necessaries and with superfluities; when he had even had his own servingman—who had usually, of course, been a rogue. These memories brought impotent anger in their train, and his eyes filled with tears. A young woman drove towards him, whip in hand. In her little cart, amid sacks and various odds and ends, lay her husband, drunk and snoring. Casanova strode by beneath the chestnut trees that lined the highway, his face working with wrath, unintelligible phrases hissing from between his clenched teeth. The woman glanced at him inquisitively and mockingly at first, then, on encountering an angry glare, with some alarm, and finally, after she had passed, there was amorous invitation in the look she gave him over her shoulder. Casanova, who was well aware that rage and hatred can assume the semblance of youth more readily than can gentleness and amiability, was prompt to realize that a bold response on his part would bring the cart to a standstill, and that the young woman would be ready to give him any assignation he pleased. Nevertheless, although the recognition of this fact put him in a better humor for the nonce, it seemed hardly worth while to waste minutes upon so trivial an adventure. He was content, therefore, to allow the peasant woman to drive her cart and all its contents unimpeded through the dust of the roadway.

The sun was now high in the heavens, and the shade of the trees hardly tempered the heat. Casanova was soon compelled to moderate his pace.

Under the thick powder of dust the shabbiness of his garments was no longer apparent, so that by his dress and bearing he might easily have been taken for a gentleman of station who had been pleased for once in a way to walk instead of drive. He had almost reached the arched gateway near his inn, when he met a heavy country carriage lumbering along the road. In it was seated a stoutish man, well dressed, and still fairly young. His hands were clasped across his stomach, his eyelids drooped, and he seemed about to doze off, when of a sudden he caught sight of Casanova, and a great change took place in him. His whole aspect betrayed great excitement. He sprang to his feet, but too quickly, and fell back into his seat. Rising again, he gave the driver a punch in the back, to make the fellow pull up. But since the carriage did not stop instantly, the passenger turned round so as not to lose sight of Casanova, signalled with both hands, and finally called to him thrice by name, in a thin, clear voice. Not till he heard the voice, did Casanova recognize who it was. By now the carriage had stopped, and Casanova smilingly seized two hands outstretched towards him, saying:

"Olivo, is it really you?"

"Yes, Signor Casanova, it is I. You recognize me, then?"

"Why not? Since I last saw you, on your wedding day, you've put on flesh; but very likely I've changed a good deal, too, in these fifteen years, though not perhaps in the same fashion."

"Not a bit of it," exclaimed Olivo. "Why, Signor Casanova, you have hardly changed at all! And it is more than fifteen years; the sixteen years were up a few days ago. As you can imagine, Amalia and I had a good talk about you on the anniversary of our wedding."

"Indeed?" said Casanova cordially. "You both think of me at times?"

The tears came to Olivo's eyes. He was still holding Casanova's hands, and he pressed them fondly.

"We have so much to thank you for, Signor Casanova. How could we ever forget our benefactor? Should we do so..."

"Don't speak of it," interrupted Casanova. "How is Signora Amalia? Do you know, I have been living in Mantua three months, very quietly to be sure, but taking plenty of walks as I always have done. How is it, Olivo, that I never met you or your wife before?"

"The matter is simple, Signor Casanova. Both Amalia and I detest the town, and we gave up living there a long time ago. Would you do me the favor to jump in? We shall be at home in an hour."

Casanova tried to excuse himself, but Olivo insisted.

"I will take no denial. How delighted Amalia will be to see you once more, and how proud to show you our three children. Yes, we have three, Signor Casanova. All girls. Thirteen, ten, and eight—not one of them old enough yet—you'll excuse me, won't you—to have her head turned by Casanova."

He laughed good-humoredly, and made as if to help Casanova into the carriage. The latter shook his head. He had been tempted for a moment by natural curiosity to accept Olivo's invitation. Then his impatience returned in full force, and he assured his would-be host that unfortunately urgent business called him away from Mantua that very afternoon.

What could he expect to find in Olivo's house? Sixteen years were a long time! Amalia would be no younger and no prettier. At his age, a girl of thirteen would not find him interesting. Olivo, too, whom he had known in old days as a lean and eager student, was now a portly, countrified paterfamilias. The proposed visit did not offer sufficient attractions to induce Casanova to abandon a journey that was to bring him thirty or forty miles nearer to Venice.

Olivo, however, was disinclined to take no for an answer. Casanova must at least accept a lift back to the inn, a kindly suggestion that could not decently be refused. It was only a few minutes' drive. The hostess, a buxom woman in the middle thirties, welcomed Casanova with a glance that did not fail to disclose to Olivo the tender relationship between the pair. She shook hands with Olivo as an old acquaintance. She was a customer of Signor Olivo's, she explained to Casanova, for an excellent medium-dry wine grown on his estate.

Olivo hastened to announce that the Chevalier de Seingalt (the hostess had addressed Casanova by this title, and Olivo promptly followed suit) was so churlish as to refuse the invitation of an old friend, on the ridiculous plea that to-day of all days he had to leave Mantua. The woman's look of gloom convinced Olivo that this was the first she had heard of Casanova's intended departure, and the latter felt it desirable to explain that his mention of the journey had been a mere pretext, lest he should incommode his friend's household by an unexpected visit, and that he had, in fact, an important piece of writing to finish during the next few days, and no place was better suited for the work than the inn, where his room was agreeably cool and quiet.

Olivo protested that the Chevalier de Seingalt would do his modest home the greatest possible honor by finishing the work in question there. A change to the country could not but be helpful in such an undertaking. If Casanova should need learned treatises and works of reference, there would be no lack of them, for Olivo's niece, the daughter of a deceased half-brother, a girl who though young was extremely erudite, had arrived a few weeks before with a whole trunkful of books. Should any guests drop in at times of an evening, the Chevalier need not put himself about—unless, indeed, after the labors of the day, cheerful conversation or a game of cards might offer welcome distraction. Directly Casanova heard of the niece, he decided he would like to make her acquaintance, and after a show of further reluctance he yielded to Olivo's solicitation, declaring, however, that on no account would he be able to leave Mantua for more than a day or two. He begged the hostess to forward promptly by messenger any letters that should arrive during his absence, since they might be of the first importance.

Matters having thus been arranged to Olivo's complete satisfaction, Casanova went to his room, made ready for the journey, and returned to the parlor in a quarter of an hour. Olivo, meanwhile, had been having a lively business talk with the hostess. He now rose, drank off his glass of wine, and with a significant wink promised to bring the Chevalier back, not perhaps to-morrow or the day after, but in any case in good order and condition. Casanova, however, had suddenly grown distrait and irritable. So cold was his farewell to the fond hostess that, at the carriage door, she whispered a parting word in his ear which was anything but amiable.

During the drive along the dusty road beneath the glare of the noonday sun, Olivo gave a garrulous and somewhat incoherent account of his life since the friends' last meeting. Shortly after his marriage he had bought a plot of land near the town, and had started in a small way as market gardener. Doing well at this trade, he had gradually been able to undertake more ambitious farming ventures. At length, under God's favor, and thanks to his own and his wife's efficiency, he had been able three years earlier to buy from the pecuniarily embarrassed Count Marazzani the latter's old and somewhat dilapidated country seat with a vineyard attached. He, his wife, and his children were comfortably settled upon this patrician estate, though with no pretence to patrician splendor. All these successes were ultimately due to the hundred and fifty gold pieces that Casanova had presented to Amalia, or rather to her mother. But for this magical aid, Olivo's lot would still have been the same. He would still have been giving instruction in reading and writing to ill-behaved youngsters. Most likely, he would have been an old bachelor and Amalia an old maid.

Casanova let him ramble on without paying much heed. The incident was one among many of the date to which it belonged. As he turned it over in his mind, it seemed to him the most trivial of them all, it had hardly even troubled the waters of memory.

He had been travelling from Rome to Turin or Paris—he had forgotten which. During a brief stay in Mantua, he caught sight of Amalia in church one morning. Pleased with her appearance, with her handsome but pale and somewhat woebegone face, he gallantly addressed her a friendly question. In those days everyone had been complaisant to Casanova. Gladly opening her heart to him, the girl told him that she was not well off; that she was in love with an usher who was likewise poor; that his father and her own mother were both unwilling to give their consent to so inauspicious a union. Casanova promptly declared himself ready to help matters on. He sought an introduction to Amalia's mother, a good-looking widow of thirty-six who was still quite worthy of being courted. Ere long Casanova was on such intimate terms with her that his word was law. When her consent to the match had been won, Olivo's father, a merchant in reduced circumstances, was no longer adverse, being specially influenced by the fact that Casanova (presented to him as a distant relative of the bride's mother) undertook to defray the expenses of the wedding and to provide part of the dowry. To Amalia, her generous patron seemed like a messenger from a higher world. She showed her gratitude in the manner prompted by her own heart. When, the evening before her wedding, she withdrew with glowing cheeks from Casanova's last embrace, she was far from thinking that she had done any wrong to her future husband, who after all owed his happiness solely to the amiability and open-handedness of this marvellous friend. Casanova had never troubled himself as to whether Amalia had confessed to Olivo the length to which she had gone in gratitude to her benefactor; whether, perchance, Olivo had taken her sacrifice as a matter of course, and had not considered it any reason for retrospective jealousy; or whether Olivo had always remained in ignorance of the matter. Nor did Casanova allow these questions to harass his mind to-day.

The heat continued to increase. The carriage, with bad springs and hard cushions, jolted the occupants abominably. Olivo went on chattering in his high, thin voice; talking incessantly of the fertility of his land, the excellencies of his wife, the good behavior of his children, and the innocent pleasures of intercourse with his neighbors—farmers and landed gentry. Casanova was bored. He began to ask himself irritably why on earth he had accepted an invitation which could bring nothing but petty vexations, if not positive disagreeables. He thought longingly of the cool parlor in Mantua, where at this very hour he might have been working unhindered at his polemic against Voltaire. He had already made up his mind to get out at an inn now in sight, hire whatever conveyance might be available, and drive back to the town, when Olivo uttered a loud "Hullo!" A pony trap suddenly pulled up, and their own carriage came to a halt, as if by mutual understanding. Three young girls sprang out, moving with such activity that the knife-board on which they had been sitting flew into the air and was overturned.

"My daughters," said Olivo, turning to Casanova with a proprietary air.

Casanova promptly moved as if to relinquish his seat in the carriage.

"Stay where you are, my dear Chevalier," said Olivo. "We shall be at home in a quarter of an hour, and for that little while we can all make shift together. Maria, Nanetta, Teresina, this is the Chevalier de Seingalt, an old friend of mine. Shake hands with him. But for him you would...."

He broke off, and whispered to Casanova: "I was just going to say something foolish."

Amending his phrase, he said: "But for him, things would have been very different!"

Like their father, the girls had black hair and dark eyes. All of them including Teresina, the eldest, who was still quite the child, looked at the stranger with frank rustic curiosity. Casanova did not stand upon ceremony; he kissed each of the girls upon either cheek. Olivo said a word or two to the lad who was driving the trap in which the children had come, and the fellow whipped up the pony and drove along the road towards Mantua.

Laughing and joking, the girls took possession of the seat opposite Olivo and Casanova. They were closely packed; they all spoke at once; and since their father likewise went on talking, Casanova found it far from easy at first to follow the conversation. One name caught his ear, that of Lieutenant Lorenzi. Teresina explained that the Lieutenant had passed them on horseback not long before, had said he intended to call in the evening, and had sent his respects to Father. Mother had at first meant to come with them to meet Father, but as it was so frightfully hot she had thought it better to stay at home with Marcolina. As for Marcolina, she was still in bed when they left home. When they came along the garden path they had pelted her with hazel nuts through the open window, or she would still be asleep.

"That's not Marcolina's way," said Olivo to his guest. "Generally she is at work in the garden at six or even earlier, and sits over her books till dinner time.

Of course we had visitors yesterday, and were up later than usual. We had a mild game of cards—not the sort of game you are used to, for we are innocent folk and don't want to win money from one another. Besides, our good Abbate usually takes a hand, so you can imagine, Chevalier, that we don't play for high stakes."

At the mention of the Abbate, the three girls laughed again, had an anecdote to tell, and this made them laugh more than ever. Casanova nodded amicably, without paying much attention. In imagination he saw Marcolina, as yet unknown to him, lying in her white bed, opposite the window. She had thrown off the bedclothes; her form was half revealed; still heavy with sleep she moved her hands to ward off the hail of nuts. His senses flamed. He was as certain that Marcolina and Lieutenant Lorenzi were in love with one another as if he had seen them in a passionate embrace. He was just as ready to detest the unknown Lorenzi as to long for the never seen Marcolina.

Through the shimmering haze of noon, a small, square tower now became visible, thrusting upward through the greyish-green foliage. The carriage turned into a by-road. To the left were vineyards rising on a gentle slope; to the right the crests of ancient trees showed above the wall of a garden. The carriage halted at a doorway in the wall. The weather-worn door stood wide. The passengers alighted, and at the master's nod the coachman drove away to the stable. A broad path led through a chestnut avenue to the house, which at first sight had an almost neglected appearance. Casanova's attention was especially attracted by a broken window in the first story. Nor did it escape his notice that the battlements of the squat tower were crumbling in places. But the house door was gracefully carved; and directly he entered the hall it was plain that the interior was carefully kept, and was certainly in far better condition than might have been supposed from the outward aspect.

"Amalia," shouted Olivo, so loudly that the vaulted ceiling rang. "Come down as quickly as you can! I have brought a friend home with me, an old friend whom you'll be delighted to see!"

Amalia had already appeared on the stairs, although to most of those who had just come out of the glaring sunlight she was invisible in the twilit interior. Casanova, whose keen vision enabled him to see well even in the dark, had noted her presence sooner than Olivo. He smiled, and was aware that the smile made him look younger. Amalia had not grown fat, as he had feared. She was still slim and youthful. She recognized him instantly.

"What a pleasant surprise!" she exclaimed without the slightest embarrassment, hastening down the stairs, and offering her cheek to Casanova. The latter, nothing loath, gave her a friendly hug.

"Am I really to believe," said he, "that Maria, Nanetta, and Teresina are your very own daughters, Amalia? No doubt the passage of the years makes it possible...."

"And all the other evidence is in keeping," supplemented Olivo. "Rely upon that, Chevalier!"

Amalia let her eyes dwell reminiscently upon the guest. "I suppose," she said, "it was your meeting with the Chevalier that has made you so late, Olivo?"

"Yes, that is why I am late. But I hope there is still something to eat?"

"Marcolina and I were frightfully hungry, but of course we have waited dinner for you."

"Can you manage to wait a few minutes longer," asked Casanova, "while I get rid of the dust of the drive?"

"I will show you your room immediately," answered Olivo. "I do hope, Chevalier, you will find it to your taste; almost as much to your taste," he winked, and added in a low tone, "as your room in the inn at Mantua—though here one or two little things may be lacking."

He led the way upstairs into the gallery surrounding the hall. From one of the corners a narrow wooden stairway led into the tower. At the top, Olivo opened the door into the turret chamber, and politely invited Casanova to enter the modest guest chamber. A maidservant brought up the valise. Casanova was then left alone in a medium-sized room, simply furnished, but equipped with all necessaries. It had four tall and narrow bay-windows, commanding views to the four points of the compass, across the sunlit plain with its green vineyards, bright meadows, golden fields, white roads, light-colored houses, and dusky gardens. Casanova concerned himself little about the view, and hastened to remove the stains of travel, being impelled less by hunger than by an eager curiosity to see Marcolina face to face. He did not change, for he wished to reserve his best suit for evening wear.

# CHAPTER II.

When Casanova reentered the hall, a panelled chamber on the ground floor, there were seated at the well-furnished board, his host and hostess, their three daughters, and a young woman. She was wearing a simple grey dress of some shimmering material. She had a graceful figure. Her gaze rested on him as frankly and indifferently as if he were a member of the household, or had been a guest a hundred times before. Her face did not light up in the way to which he had grown accustomed in earlier years, when he had been a charming youth, or later in his handsome prime. But for a good while now Casanova had ceased to expect this from a new acquaintance. Nevertheless, even of late the mention of his name had usually sufficed to arouse on a woman's face an expression of tardy admiration, or at least some trace of regret, which was an admission that the hearer would have loved to meet him a few years earlier. Yet now, when Olivo introduced him to Marcolina as Signor Casanova, Chevalier de Seingalt, she smiled as she would have smiled at some utterly indifferent name that carried with it no aroma of adventure and mystery. Even when he took his seat by her side, kissed her hand, and allowed his eyes as they dwelt on her to gleam with delight and desire, her manner betrayed nothing of the demure gratification that might have seemed an appropriate answer to so ardent a wooing.

After a few polite commonplaces, Casanova told his neighbor that he had been informed of her intellectual attainments, and asked what was her chosen subject of study. Her chief interest, she rejoined, was in the higher mathematics, to which she had been introduced by Professor Morgagni, the renowned teacher at the university of Bologna. Casanova expressed his surprise that so charming a young lady should have an interest, certainly exceptional, in a dry and difficult subject. Marcolina replied that in her view the higher mathematics was the most imaginative of all the sciences; one might even say that its nature made it akin to the divine. When Casanova asked for further enlightenment upon a view so novel to him, Marcolina modestly declined to continue the topic, declaring that the others at table, and above all her uncle, would much rather hear some details of a newly recovered friend's travels than listen to a philosophical disquisition.

Amalia was prompt to second the proposal; and Casanova, always willing to oblige in this matter, said in easy-going fashion that during recent years he had been mainly engaged in secret diplomatic missions. To mention only places of importance, he had continually been going to and fro between Madrid, Paris, London, Amsterdam, and St. Petersburg. He gave an account of meetings and conversations, some grave and some gay, with men and women of all classes, and did not forget to speak of his friendly reception at the court of Catharine of Russia. He jestingly related how Frederick the Great had nearly appointed him instructor at a cadet school for Pomeranian junkers—a danger from which he had escaped by a precipitous flight. Of these and many other things he spoke as recent happenings, although in reality they had occurred years or decades before. Romancing freely, he was hardly conscious when he was lying either on a small scale or on a large, being equally delighted with his own conceits and with the pleasure he was giving to his auditors. While thus recounting real and imaginary incidents, he could almost delude himself into the belief that he was still the bold, radiant Casanova, the favorite of fortune and of beautiful women, the honored guest of secular and spiritual princes, the man whose spendings and gamblings and gifts must be reckoned in thousands. It was possible for him to forget that he was a decayed starveling, supported by pitiful remittances from former friends in England and Spain—-doles which often failed to arrive, so that he was reduced to the few and paltry gold pieces which he could win from Baron Perotti or from the Baron's guests. He could even forget that his highest aim now was to return to his natal city where he had been cast into prison and from which, since his escape, he had been banned; to return as one of the meanest of its citizens, as writer, as beggar, as nonentity; to accept so inglorious a close to a once brilliant career.

Marcolina listened attentively like the others, but with the same expression as if she had been listening to someone reading aloud from an amusing narrative. Her face did not betray the remotest realization of the fact that the speaker was Casanova; that she was listening to the man who had had all these experiences and many more; that she was sitting beside the lover of a thousand women. Very different was the fire in Amalia's eyes. To her, Casanova was the same as ever. To her, his voice was no less seductive than it had been sixteen years earlier. He could not but be aware that at a word or a sign, and as soon as he pleased, he could revive this old adventure. But what to him was Amalia at this hour, when he longed for Marcolina as he had never longed for woman before. Beneath the shimmering folds of her dress he seemed to see her naked body; her firm young breasts allured him; once when she stooped to pick up her handkerchief, Casanova's inflamed fancy made him attach so ardent a significance to her movement that he felt near to swooning. Marcolina did not fail to notice the involuntary pause in the flow of his conversation; she perceived that his gaze had begun to flicker strangely. In her countenance he could read a sudden hostility, a protest, a trace of disgust.

Casanova speedily recovered his self-command, and was about to continue his reminiscences with renewed vigor, when a portly priest entered. Olivo introduced him as Abbate Rossi, and Casanova at once recognized him as the man he had met twenty-seven years earlier upon a market boat plying between Venice and Chioggia.

"You had one eye bandaged," said Casanova, who rarely missed a chance of showing off his excellent memory. "A young peasant-woman wearing a yellow kerchief round her head advised you to use a healing unguent which an apothecary with an exceedingly hoarse voice happened to have with him."

The Abbate nodded, and smiled, well-pleased. Then, with a sly expression, he came quite close to Casanova, as if about to tell him a secret. But he spoke out loud.

"As for you, Signor Casanova, you were with a wedding party. I don't know whether you were one of the ordinary guests or whether you were best man, but I remember that the bride looked at you far more languishingly than at the bridegroom. The wind rose; there was half a gale; you began to read a risky poem."

"No doubt the Chevalier only did so in order to lay the storm," said Marcolina.

"I never claim the powers of a wizard," rejoined Casanova. "But I will not deny that after I had begun to read, no one bothered about the storm." The three girls had encircled the Abbate. For an excellent reason. From his capacious pockets he produced quantities of luscious sweets, and popped them into the children's mouths with his stumpy fingers. Meanwhile Olivo gave the newcomer a circumstantial account of the rediscovery of Casanova. Dreamily Amalia continued to gaze at the beloved guest's masterful brown forehead.

The children ran out into the garden; Marcolina had risen from the table and was watching them through the open window. The Abbate had brought a message from the Marchese Celsi, who proposed to call that evening, with his wife, upon his dear friend Olivo.

"Excellent," said Olivo. "We shall have a pleasant game of cards in honor of the Chevalier. I am expecting the two Ricardis; and Lorenzi is also coming—the girls met him out riding this morning."

"Is he still here?" asked the Abbate. "A week ago I was told he had to rejoin his regiment."

"I expect the Marchesa got him an extension of leave from the Colonel."

"I am surprised," interjected Casanova, "that any Mantuese officers can get leave at present." He went on: "Two friends of mine, one from Mantua and the other from Cremona, left last night with their regiments, marching towards Milan."

"Has war broken out?" inquired Marcolina from the window. She had turned round; her face betrayed nothing, but there was a slight quaver in her voice which no one but Casanova noticed.

"It may come to nothing," he said lightly. "But the Spaniards seem rather bellicose, and it is necessary to be on the alert."

Olivo looked important and wrinkled his brow. "Does anyone know," he asked, "whether we shall side with Spain or with France?"

"I don't think Lieutenant Lorenzi will care a straw about that," suggested the Abbate. "All he wants is a chance to prove his military prowess."

"He has done so already," said Amalia. "He was in the battle at Pavia three years ago."

Marcolina said not a word.

Casanova knew enough. He went to the window beside Marcolina and looked out into the garden. He saw nothing but the wide greensward where the children were playing. It was surrounded by a close-set row of stately trees within the encompassing wall.

"What lovely grounds," he said, turning to Olivo. "I should so like to have a look at them."

"Nothing would please me better, Chevalier," answered Olivo, "than to show you my vineyards and the rest of my estate. You need only ask Amalia, and she will tell you that during the years since I bought this little place I have had no keener desire than to welcome you as guest upon my own land and under my own roof. Ten times at least I was on the point of writing you an invitation, but was always withheld by the doubt whether my letter would reach you. If I did happen to hear from some one that he had recently seen you in Lisbon, I could be quite sure that in the interval you would have left for Warsaw or Vienna. Now, when as if by miracle I have caught you on the point of quitting Mantua, and when—I can assure you, Amalia, it was no easy matter—I have succeeded in enticing you here, you are so niggard with your time that—would you believe it, Signor Abbate, he refuses to spare us more than a couple of days!"

"Perhaps the Chevalier will allow himself to be persuaded to prolong his visit," said the Abbate, who was contentedly munching a huge mouthful of peach. As he spoke, he glanced at Amalia in a way that led Casanova to infer that his hostess had told the Abbate more than she had told her husband.

"I fear that will be quite impossible," said Casanova with decision. "I need not conceal from friends who are so keenly interested in my fortunes, that my Venetian fellow-citizens are on the point of atoning for the injustice of earlier years. The atonement comes rather late, but is all the more honorable. I should seem ungrateful, or even rancorous, were I to resist their importunities any longer." With a wave of his hand he warded off an eager but respectful enquiry which he saw taking shape upon his host's lips, and hastened to remark: "Well, Olivo, I am ready. Show me your little kingdom."

"Would it not be wiser," interposed Amalia, "to wait until it is cooler? I am sure the Chevalier would prefer to rest for a while, or to stroll in the shade." Her eyes sought Casanova's with shy entreaty, as if she thought her fate would be decided once again during such a walk in the garden.

No one had anything to say against Amalia's suggestion, and they all went out of doors. Marcolina, who led the way, ran across the sunlit greensward to join the children in their game of battledore and shuttlecock. She was hardly taller than the eldest of the three girls; and when her hair came loose in the exercise and floated over her shoulders she too looked like a child. Olivo and the Abbate seated themselves on a stone bench beneath the trees, not far from the house. Amalia sauntered on with Casanova. As soon as the two were out of hearing, she began to converse with Casanova in a tone which seemed to ignore the lapse of years.

"So we meet again, Casanova! How I have longed for this day. I never doubted its coming."

"A mere chance has brought me," said Casanova coldly.

Amalia smiled. "Have it your own way," she said. "Anyhow, you are here! All these sixteen years I have done nothing but dream of this day!"

"I can't help thinking," countered Casanova, "that throughout the long interval you must have dreamed of many other things—and must have done more than dream."

Amalia shook her head. "You know better, Casanova. Nor had you forgotten me, for were it otherwise, in your eagerness to get to Venice, you would never have accepted Olivo's invitation."

"What do you mean, Amalia? Can you imagine I have come here to betray your husband?"

"How can you use such a phrase, Casanova? Were I to be yours once again, there would be neither betrayal nor sin."

Casanova laughed. "No sin? Wherefore not? Because I'm an old man?"

"You are not old. For me you can never be an old man. In your arms I had my first taste of bliss, and I doubt not it is my destiny that my last bliss shall be shared with you!"

"Your last?" rejoined Casanova cynically, though he was not altogether unmoved. "I think my friend Olivo would have a word to say about that."

"What you speak of," said Amalia reddening, "is duty, and even pleasure; but it is not and never has been bliss."

They did not walk to the end of the grass alley. Both seemed to shun the neighborhood of the greensward, where Marcolina and the children were playing. As if by common consent they retraced their steps, and, silent now, approached the house again. One of the ground-floor windows at the gable end of the house was open. Through this Casanova glimpsed in the dark interior a half-drawn curtain, from behind which the foot of a bed projected. Over an adjoining chair was hanging a light, gauzy dress.

"Is that Marcolina's room?" enquired Casanova.

Amalia nodded. "Do you like her?" she said—nonchalantly, as it seemed to Casanova.

"Of course, since she is good looking."

"She's a good girl as well."

Casanova shrugged, as if the goodness were no concern of his. Then: "Tell me, Amalia, did you think me still handsome when you first saw me to-day?"

"I do not know if your looks have changed. To me you seem just the same as of old. You are as I have always seen you, as I have seen you in my dreams."

"Look well, Amalia. See the wrinkles on my forehead; the loose folds of my neck; the crow's-feet round my eyes. And look," he grinned, "I have lost one of my eye teeth. Look at these hands, too, Amalia. My fingers are like claws; there are yellow spots on the finger-nails; the blue veins stand out. They are the hands of an old man."

She clasped both his hands as he held them out for her to see, and affectionately kissed them one after the other in the shaded walk. "To-night, I will kiss you on the lips," she said, with a mingling of humility and tenderness, which roused his gall.

Close by, where the alley opened on to the greensward, Marcolina was stretched on the grass, her hands clasped beneath her head, looking skyward while the shuttlecocks flew to and fro. Suddenly reaching upwards, she seized one of them in mid air, and laughed triumphantly. The girls flung themselves upon her as she lay defenceless.

Casanova thrilled. "Neither my lips nor my hands are yours to kiss. Your waiting for me and your dreams of me will prove to have been vain—unless I should first make Marcolina mine."

"Are you mad, Casanova?" exclaimed Amalia, with distress in her voice.

"If I am, we are both on the same footing," replied Casanova. "You are mad because in me, an old man, you think that you can rediscover the beloved of your youth; I am mad because I have taken it into my head that I wish to possess Marcolina. But perhaps we shall both be restored to reason. Marcolina shall restore me to youth—for you. So help me to my wishes, Amalia!"

"You are really beside yourself, Casanova. What you ask is impossible. She will have nothing to do with any man."

Casanova laughed. "What about Lieutenant Lorenzi?"

"Lorenzi? What do you mean?"

"He is her lover. I am sure of it."

"You are utterly mistaken. He asked for her hand, and she rejected his proposal. Yet he is young and handsome. I almost think him handsomer than you ever were, Casanova!"

"He was a suitor for her hand?"

"Ask Olivo if you don't believe me."

"Well, what do I care about that? What care I whether she be virgin or strumpet, wife or widow—I want to make her mine!"

"I can't give her to you, my friend!" Amalia's voice expressed genuine concern.

"You see for yourself," he said, "what a pitiful creature I have become. Ten years ago, five years ago, I should have needed neither helper nor advocate, even though Marcolina had been the very goddess of virtue. And now I am trying to make you play the procuress. If I were only a rich man. Had I but ten thousand ducats. But I have not even ten. I am a beggar, Amalia."

"Had you a hundred thousand, you could not buy Marcolina. What does she care about money? She loves books, the sky, the meadows, butterflies, playing with children. She has inherited a small competence which more than suffices for her needs."

"Were I but a sovereign prince," cried Casanova, somewhat theatrically, as was his wont when strongly moved. "Had I but the power to commit men to prison, to send them to the scaffold. But I am nothing. A beggar, and a liar into the bargain. I importune the Supreme Council for a post, a crust of bread, a home! What a poor thing have I become! Are you not sickened by me, Amalia?"

"I love you, Casanova!"

"Then give her to me, Amalia. It rests with you, I am confident. Tell her what you please. Say I have threatened you. Say you think I am capable of setting fire to the house. Say I am a fool, a dangerous lunatic escaped from an asylum, but that the embraces of a virgin will restore me to sanity. Yes, tell her that."

"She does not believe in miracles."

"Does not believe in miracles? Then she does not believe in God either. So much the better! I have influence with the Archbishop of Milan. Tell her so. I can ruin her. I can destroy you all. It is true, Amalia. What books does she read? Doubtless some of them are on the Index. Let me see them. I will compile a list. A hint from me...."

"Not a word more, Casanova! Here she comes. Keep yourself well in hand; do not let your eyes betray you. Listen, Casanova; I have never known a purer-minded girl. Did she suspect what I have heard from you, she would feel herself soiled, and for the rest of your stay she would not so much as look at you. Talk to her; talk to her. You will soon ask her pardon and mine."

Marcolina came up with the girls, who ran on into the house. She paused, as if out of courtesy to the guest, standing before him, while Amalia deliberately withdrew. Indeed, it actually seemed to Casanova that from those pale, half-parted lips, from the smooth brow crowned with light-brown hair now restored to order, there emanated an aroma of aloofness and purity. Rarely had he had this feeling with regard to any woman; nor had he had it in the case of Marcolina when they were within four walls. A devotional mood, a spirit of self-sacrifice knowing nothing of desire, seemed to take possession of his soul. Discreetly, in a respectful tone such as at that day was customary towards persons of rank, in a manner which she could not but regard as flattering, he enquired whether it was her purpose to resume her studies that evening. She answered that in the country her work was somewhat irregular. Nevertheless, even during free hours, mathematical problems upon which she had recently been pondering, would at times invade her mind unawares. This had just happened while she was lying on the greensward gazing up into the sky.

Casanova, emboldened by the friendliness of her demeanor, asked jestingly what was the nature of this lofty, urgent problem. She replied, in much the same tone, that it had nothing whatever to do with the Cabala, with which, so rumor ran, the Chevalier de Seingalt worked wonders. He would therefore not know what to make of her problem.

Casanova was piqued that she should speak of the Cabala with such unconcealed contempt. In his rare hours of heart-searching he was well aware that the mystical system of numbers which passed by that name had neither sense nor purpose. He knew it had no correspondence with any natural reality; that it was no more than an instrument whereby cheats and jesters—Casanova assumed these rôles by turn, and was a master player in both capacities—could lead credulous fools by the nose. Nevertheless, in defiance of his own better judgment, he now undertook to defend the Cabala as a serious and perfectly valid science. He spoke of the divine nature of the number seven, to which there are so many references in Holy Writ; of the deep prophetic significance of pyramids of figures, for the construction of which he had himself invented a new system; and of the frequent fulfilment of the forecasts he had based upon this system. In Amsterdam, a few years ago, through the use of arithmancy, he had induced Hope the banker to take over the insurance of a ship which was already reported lost, whereby the banker had made two hundred thousand gold guilders. He held forth so eloquently in defence of his preposterous theories that, as often happened, he began to believe all the nonsense he was talking. At length he went so far as to maintain that the Cabala was not so much a branch of mathematics as the metaphysical perfectionment of mathematics.

At this point, Marcolina, who had been listening attentively and with apparent seriousness, suddenly assumed a half-commiserating, half-mischievous expression, and said:

"You are trying, Signor Casanova"—she seemed deliberately to avoid addressing him as Chevalier—"to give me an elaborate proof of your renowned talent as entertainer, and I am extremely grateful to you. But of course you know as well as I do that the Cabala has not merely nothing to do with mathematics, but is in conflict with the very essence of mathematics. The Cabala bears to mathematics the same sort of relationship that the confused or fallacious chatter of the Sophists bore to the serene, lofty doctrines of Plato and of Aristotle."

"Nevertheless, beautiful and learned Marcolina, you will admit," answered Casanova promptly, "that even the Sophists were far from being such contemptible, foolish apprentices as your harsh criticism would imply. Let me give you a contemporary example. M. Voltaire's whole technique of thought and writing entitles us to describe him as an Arch-Sophist. Yet no one will refuse the due meed of honor to his extraordinary talent. I would not myself refuse it, though I am at this moment engaged in composing a polemic against him. Let me add that I am not allowing myself to be influenced in his favor by recollection of the extreme civility he was good enough to show me when I visited him at Ferney ten years ago."

"It is really most considerate of you to be so lenient in your criticism of the greatest mind of the century!" Marcolina smilingly retorted.

"A great mind—the greatest of the century!" exclaimed Casanova. "To give him such a designation seems to me inadmissible, were it only because, for all his genius, he is an ungodly man—nay positively an atheist. No atheist can be a man of great mind."

"As I see the matter, there is no such incompatibility. But the first thing you have to prove is your title to describe Voltaire as an atheist."

Casanova was now in his element. In the opening chapter of his polemic he had cited from Voltaire's works, especially from the famous *Pucelle,* a number of passages that seemed peculiarly well-fitted to justify the charge of atheism. Thanks to his unfailing memory, he was able to repeat these citations verbatim, and to marshal his own counter-arguments. But in Marcolina he had to cope with an opponent who was little inferior to himself in extent of knowledge and mental acumen; and who, moreover, excelled him, not perhaps in fluency of speech, but at any rate in artistry of presentation and clarity of expression. The passages Casanova had selected as demonstrating Voltaire's spirit of mockery, his scepticism, and his atheism, were adroitly interpreted by Marcolina as testifying to the Frenchman's scientific genius, to his skill as an author, and to his indefatigable ardor in the search for truth. She boldly contended that doubt, mockery, nay unbelief itself, if associated with such a wealth of knowledge, such absolute honesty, and such high courage, must be more pleasing to God than the humility of the pious, which was apt to be a mask for lack of capacity to think logically, and often enough—there were plenty of examples—a mask for cowardice and hypocrisy.

Casanova listened with growing astonishment. He felt quite incompetent to convert Marcolina to his own way of thinking; all the more as he increasingly realized that her counterstrokes were threatening to demolish the tottering intellectual edifice which, of late years, he had been accustomed to mistake for faith. He took refuge in the trite assertion that such views as Marcolina's were a menace, not only to the ecclesiastical ordering of society, but to the very foundations of social life. This enabled him to make a clever change of front, to pass into the field of politics, where he hoped that his wide experience and his knowledge of the world would render it possible for him to get the better of his adversary. But although she lacked acquaintance with the notable personalities of the age; although she was without inside knowledge of courtly and diplomatic intrigues; although, therefore, she had to renounce any attempt to answer Casanova in detail, even when she felt there was good reason to distrust the accuracy of his assertions—nevertheless, it was clear to him from the tenor of her remarks, that she had little respect for the princes of the earth or for the institutions of state; and she made no secret of her conviction that, alike in small things and in great, the world was not so much a world ruled by selfishness and lust for power, as a world in a condition of hopeless confusion. Rarely had Casanova encountered such freedom of thought in women; never had he met with anything of the kind in a girl who was certainly not yet twenty years old. It was painful to him to remember that in earlier and better days his own mind had with deliberate, self-complacent boldness moved along the paths whereon Marcolina was now advancing—although in her case there did not seem to exist any consciousness of exceptional courage. Fascinated by the uniqueness of her methods of thought and expression, he almost forgot that he was walking beside a young, beautiful, desirable woman, a forgetfulness all the more remarkable as the two were alone in the leafy alley, and at a considerable distance from the house.

Suddenly, breaking off in the middle of a sentence, Marcolina joyfully exclaimed, "Here comes my uncle!"

Casanova, as if he had to rectify an omission, whispered in her ear: "What a nuisance. I should have liked to go on talking to you for hours, Marcolina." He was aware that his eyes were again lighting up with desire.

At this Marcolina, who in the spirited exchange of their recent conversation had almost abandoned her defensive attitude, displayed a renewed reserve. Her expression manifested the same protest, the same repulsion, which had wounded Casanova earlier in the day.

"Am I really so repulsive?" he anxiously asked himself. Then, replying in thought to his own question: "No, that is not the reason. Marcolina is not really a woman. She is a she-professor, a she-philosopher, one of the wonders of the world perhaps—but not a woman."

Yet even as he mused, he knew he was merely attempting to deceive himself, console himself, save himself; and all his endeavors were vain.

Olivo, who had now come up, addressed Marcolina. "Have I not done well to invite some one here with whom you can converse as learnedly as with your professors at Bologna?"

"Indeed, Uncle," answered Marcolina, "there was not one of them who would have ventured to challenge Voltaire to a duel!"

"What, Voltaire? The Chevalier has called him out?" cried Olivo, misunderstanding the jest.

"Your witty niece, Olivo, refers to the polemic on which I have been at work for the last few days, the pastime of leisure hours. I used to have weightier occupations."

Marcolina, ignoring this remark, said: "You will find it pleasantly cool now for your walk. Goodbye for the present." She nodded a farewell, and moved briskly across the greensward to the house.

Casanova, repressing an impulse to follow her with his eyes, enquired: "Is Signora Amalia coming with us?"

"No, Chevalier," answered Olivo. "She has a number of things to attend to in the house; and besides, this is the girls' lesson time."

"What an excellent housewife and mother! You're a lucky fellow, Olivo!"

"I tell myself the same thing every day," responded Olivo, with tears in his eyes.

They passed by the gable end of the house. Marcolina's window was still open; the pale, diaphanous gown showed up against the dark background of the room. Along the wide chestnut avenue they made their way on to the road, now completely in the shade. Leisurely, they walked up the slope skirting the garden wall. Where it ended, the vineyard began. Between tall poles, from which purple clusters hung, Olivo led his guest to the summit. With a complacent air of ownership, he waved towards the house, lying at the foot of the hill. Casanova fancied he could detect a female figure flitting to and fro in the turret chamber.

The sun was near to setting, but the heat was still considerable. Beads of perspiration coursed down Olivo's cheeks, but Casanova's brow showed no trace of moisture. Strolling down the farther slope, they reached an olive grove. From tree to tree vines were trained trellis-wise, while between the rows of olive trees golden ears of corn swayed in the breeze.

"In a thousand ways," said Casanova appreciatively, "the sun brings increase."

With even greater wealth of detail than before, Olivo recounted how he had acquired this fine estate, and how two great vintage years and two good harvests had made him a well-to-do, in fact a wealthy, man.

Casanova pursued the train of his own thoughts, attending to Olivo's narrative only in so far as was requisite to enable him from time to time to interpose a polite question or to make an appropriate comment. Nothing claimed his interest until Olivo, after talking of all and sundry, came back to the topic of his family, and at length to Marcolina. But Casanova learned little that was new. She had lost her mother early. Her father, Olivo's half-brother, had been a physician in Bologna. Marcolina, while still a child, had astonished everyone by her precocious intelligence; but the marvel was soon staled by custom. A few years later, her father died. Since then she had been an inmate in the household of a distinguished professor at the university of Bologna, Morgagni to wit, who hoped that his pupil would become a woman of great learning. She always spent the summer with her uncle. There had been several proposals for her hand; one from a Bolognese merchant; one from a neighboring landowner; and lastly the proposal of Lieutenant Lorenzi. She had refused them all, and it seemed to be her design to devote her whole life to the service of knowledge. As Olivo rambled on with his story, Casanova's desires grew beyond measure, while the recognition that these desires were utterly foolish and futile reduced him almost to despair.

# CHAPTER III.

Casanova and Olivo regained the highroad. In a cloud of dust, a carriage drove up, and as they drew near the occupants shouted greetings. The newcomers were an elderly gentleman in elegant attire and a lady who was somewhat younger, of generous proportions, and conspicuously rouged.

"The Marchese," whispered Olivo to his companion.

The carriage halted.

"Good evening, my dear Olivo," said the Marchese. "Will you be so good as to introduce me to the Chevalier de Seingalt? I have no doubt that it is the Chevalier whom I have the pleasure of seeing."

Casanova bowed, saying: "Yes, I am he."

"I am the Marchese Celsi. Let me present the Marchesa, my spouse." The lady offered her finger tips. Casanova touched them with his lips.

The Marchese was two or three inches taller than Casanova, and unnaturally lean. He had a narrow face, of a yellow, waxy tint; his greenish eyes were piercing; his thick eyebrows were of reddish color, and met across the root of the nose. These characteristics gave him a somewhat formidable aspect. "My good Olivo," he said, "we are all going to the same destination. Since it is little more than half a mile to your house, I shall get out and walk with you. You won't mind driving the rest of the way alone," he added, turning to the Marchesa, who had meanwhile been gazing at Casanova with searching, passionate eyes. Without awaiting his wife's answer, the Marchese nodded to the coachman, who promptly lashed the horses furiously, as if he had some reason for driving his mistress away at top speed. In an instant the carriage vanished in a whirl of dust.

"The whole neighborhood," said the Marchese, "is already aware that the Chevalier de Seingalt has come to spend a few days with his friend Olivo. It must be glorious to bear so renowned a name."

"You flatter me, Signor Marchese," replied Casanova. "I have not yet abandoned the hope of winning such a name, but I am still far from having done so. It may be that a work on which I am now engaged will bring me nearer to the goal."

"We can take a short cut here," said Olivo, turning into a path which led straight to the wall of his garden.

"Work?" echoed the Marchese with a doubtful air. "May I enquire to what work you refer, Chevalier?"

"If you ask me that question, Signor Marchese, I shall in my turn feel impelled to enquire what you meant just now when you referred to my renown."

Arrogantly he faced the Marchese's piercing eyes. He knew perfectly well that neither his romance *Icosameron* nor yet his *Confutazione della storia del governo veneto d'Amelot de la Houssaie* had brought him any notable reputation as an author. Nevertheless it was his pose to imply that for him no other sort of reputation was desirable. He therefore deliberately misunderstood the Marchese's tentative observations and cautious allusions, which implied that Casanova was a celebrated seducer, gamester, man of affairs, political emissary, or what not. Celsi made no reference to authorship, for he had never heard of either the *Refutation of Amelot* or the *Icosameron*. At length, therefore, in polite embarrassment, he said: "After all, there is only one Casanova."

"There, likewise, you are mistaken, Signor Marchese," said Casanova coldly. "I have relatives, and a connoisseur like yourself must surely be acquainted with the name of one of my brothers, Francesco Casanova, the painter."

It seemed that the Marchese had no claim to connoisseurship in this field either, and he turned the conversation to acquaintances living in Naples, Rome, Milan, or Mantua, persons whom Casanova was not unlikely to have met. In this connection he also mentioned the name of Baron Perotti, but somewhat contemptuously.

Casanova was constrained to admit that he often played cards at the Baron's house. "For distraction," he explained; "for half an hour's relaxation before bedtime. In general, I have given up this way of wasting my time."

"I am sorry," said the Marchese, "for I must own it has been one of the dreams of my life to cross swords with you. Not only, indeed, at the card table; for when I was younger I would gladly have been your rival in other fields. Would you believe it—I forget how long ago it was—I once entered Spa on the very day, at the very hour, when you left the place. Our carriages must have passed one another on the road. In Ratisbon, too, I had the same piece of ill luck. There I actually occupied the room of which your tenancy had just expired."

"It is indeed unfortunate," said Casanova, flattered in spite of himself, "that people's paths so often cross too late in life."

"Not yet too late!" exclaimed the Marchese. "There are certain respects in which I shall not be loath to avow myself vanquished before the fight begins. But as regards games of chance, my dear Chevalier, we are perhaps both of us precisely at the age...."

Casanova cut him short. "At the age—very likely. Unfortunately, however, I can no longer look forward to the pleasure of measuring myself at the card table with a partner of your rank. The reason is simple." He spoke in the tone of a dethroned sovereign. "Despite my renown, my dear Marchese, I am now practically reduced to the condition of a beggar."

The Marchese involuntarily lowered his eyes before Casanova's haughty gaze. He shook his head incredulously, as if he had been listening to a strange jest. Olivo, who had followed the conversation with the keenest attention, and had accompanied the skilful parries of his marvellous friend with approving nods, could hardly repress a gesture of alarm. They had just reached a narrow wooden door in the garden wall. Olivo produced a key, and turned the creaking lock. Giving the Marchese precedence into the garden, he arrested Casanova by the arm, whispering:

"You must take back those last words, Chevalier, before you set foot in my house again. The money I have been owing you these sixteen years awaits you. I was only afraid to speak of it. Amalia will tell you. It is counted out and ready. I had proposed to hand it over to you on your departure...."

Casanova gently interrupted him. "You owe me nothing, Olivo. You know perfectly well that those paltry gold pieces were a wedding present from the friend of Amalia's mother. Please drop the subject. What are a few ducats to me?" He raised his voice as he spoke, so that the Marchese, who had paused at a few paces' distance could hear the concluding words. "I stand at a turning-point in my fortunes."

Olivo exchanged glances with Casanova, as if asking permission, and then explained to the Marchese: "You must know that the Chevalier has been summoned to Venice, and will set out for home in a few days."

"I would rather put it," remarked Casanova as they approached the house, "that summonses, growing ever more urgent, have been reaching me for a considerable while. But it seems to me that the senators took long enough to make up their minds, and may in their turn practise the virtue of patience."

"Unquestionably," said the Marchese, "you are entitled to stand upon your dignity, Chevalier."

They emerged from the avenue on to the greensward, across which the shadow of the house had now lengthened. Close to the dwelling, the rest of the little company was awaiting them. All rose and came to meet them. The Abbate led the way, with Marcolina and Amalia on either side. They were followed by the Marchesa, with whom came a tall, young officer, clad in a red uniform trimmed with silver lace, and wearing jack-boots—evidently Lorenzi. As he spoke to the Marchesa, he scanned her powdered shoulders as if they were well-known samples of other beauties with which he was equally familiar. The Marchesa smiled up at him beneath half-closed lids. Even a tyro in such matters could hardly fail to realize the nature of their relationship, or to perceive that they were quite unconcerned at its disclosure. They were conversing in animated fashion, but in low tones; and they ceased talking only when they caught up with the others.

Olivo introduced Casanova and Lorenzi to one another. They exchanged glances with a cold aloofness that seemed to offer mutual assurances of dislike; then, with a forced smile, both bowed stiffly without offering to shake hands. Lorenzi was handsome, with a narrow visage and features sharply cut for his age. At the back of his eyes something difficult to grasp seemed to lurk, something likely to suggest caution to one of experience. For a moment, Casanova was in doubt as to who it was that Lorenzi reminded him of. Then he realized that his own image stood before him, the image of himself as he had been thirty years before. "Have

I been reincarnated in his form?" Casanova asked himself. "But I must have died before that could happen." It flashed through his mind: "Have I not been dead for a long time? What is there left of the Casanova who was young, handsome, and happy?" Amalia broke in upon his musings. As if from a distance, though she stood close at hand, she asked him how he had enjoyed his walk. Raising his voice so that all could hear, he expressed his admiration for the fertile, well-managed estate.

Meanwhile upon the greensward the maidservant was laying the table for supper. The two elder girls were "helping." With much fuss and giggling, they brought out of the house the silver, the wine glasses, and other requisites.

Gradually the dusk fell; a cool breeze stirred through the garden. Marcolina went to the table, to put the finishing touches to the work of the maidservant and the girls. The others wandered about the greensward and along the alleys. The Marchesa was extremely polite to Casanova. She said that the story of his remarkable escape from The Leads in Venice was not unknown to her, but it would be a pleasure to hear it from his own lips. With a meaning smile she added that she understood him to have had far more dangerous adventures, which he might perhaps be less inclined to recount. Casanova rejoined that he had indeed had a number of lively experiences, but had never made serious acquaintance with that mode of existence whose meaning and very essence were danger. Although, many years before, during troublous times, he had for a few months been a soldier upon the island of Corfu (was there any profession on earth into which the current of fate had not drifted him?), he had never had the good fortune to go through a real campaign, such as that which, he understood, Lieutenant Lorenzi was about to experience—a piece of luck for which he was inclined to envy the Lieutenant.

"Then you know more than I do, Signor Casanova," said Lorenzi in a challenging tone. "Indeed, you are better informed than the Colonel himself, for he has just given me an indefinite extension of leave."

"Is that so?" exclaimed the Marchese, unable to master his rage. He added spitefully: "Do you know, Lorenzi, we, or rather my wife, had counted so definitely on your leaving, that we had invited one of our friends, Baldi the singer, to stay with us next week."

"No matter," rejoined Lorenzi, unperturbed. "Baldi and I are the best of friends. We shall get on famously together. You think so, don't you?" he said, turning to the Marchesa with a smile. "You'd better!" said the Marchesa, laughing gaily.

As she spoke she seated herself at the table, beside Olivo, with Lorenzi on the other hand. Opposite sat Amalia, between the Marchese and Casanova. Next to Casanova, at one end of the long, narrow table, was Marcolina; next to Olivo, at the other end, sat the Abbate. Supper, like dinner, was a simple but tasteful meal. The two elder girls, Teresina and Nanetta, waited on the guests, and served the excellent wine grown on Olivo's hillsides. Both the Marchese and the Abbate paid their thanks to the young waitresses with playful and somewhat equivocal caresses which a stricter parent than Olivo would probably have discountenanced.

Amalia seemed to be unaware of all this. She was pale, dejected, and looked like a woman determined to be old, since her own youth had ceased to interest her.

"Is this all that remains of my empire?" thought Casanova bitterly, contemplating her in profile. Yet perhaps it was the illumination which gave so gloomy a cast to Amalia's features. From the interior of the house a broad beam of light fell upon the guests. Otherwise the glimmer in the sky sufficed them. The dark crests of the trees limited the outlook; Casanova was reminded of the eerie garden in which, late one evening many years before, he had awaited the coming of his mistress.

"Murano!" he whispered to himself, and trembled. Then he spoke aloud: "On an island near Venice there is a convent garden where I last set foot several decades ago. At night, there, the scent is just like this."

"Were you ever a monk?" asked the Marchesa, sportively.

"All but," replied Casanova with a smile, explaining, truthfully enough, that when he was a lad of fifteen he had been given minor orders by the archbishop of Venice, but that before attaining full manhood he had decided to lay aside the cassock.

The Abbate mentioned that there was a nunnery close at hand, and strongly recommended Casanova to visit the place if he had never seen it. Olivo heartily endorsed the recommendation, singing the praises of the picturesque old building, the situation, and the diversified beauties of the approach.

"The Lady Abbess, Sister Serafina," continued the Abbate, "is an extremely learned woman, a duchess by birth. She has told me—by letter, of course, for the inmates are under a vow of perpetual silence—that she has heard of Marcolina's erudition, and would like to meet her face to face."

"I hope, Marcolina," said Lorenzi, speaking to her for the first time, "that you will not attempt to imitate the noble abbess in other respects as well as learning."

"Why should I?" rejoined Marcolina serenely. "We can maintain our freedom without vows. Better without than with, for a vow is a form of coercion."

Casanova was sitting next to her. He did not dare to let his foot touch hers lightly, or to press his knee against hers. He was certain that should she for the third time look at him with that expression of horror and loathing, he would be driven to some act of folly. As the meal progressed, as the number of emptied glasses grew and the conversation waxed livelier and more general, Casanova heard, once more as from afar, Amalia's voice.

"I have spoken to Marcolina."

"You have spoken to her?" A mad hope flamed up in him. "Calm yourself, Casanova. We did not speak of you, but only of her and her plans for the future. I say to you again, she will never give herself to any man."

Olivo, who had been drinking freely, suddenly rose, glass in hand, and delivered himself of a few stumbling phrases concerning the great honor conferred upon his humble home by the visit of his dear friend, the Chevalier de Seingalt.

"But where, my dear Olivo, is the Chevalier de Seingalt of whom you speak?" enquired Lorenzi in his clear, insolent voice.

Casanova's first impulse was to throw the contents of his glass in Lorenzi's face.

Amalia touched his arm lightly, to restrain him, and said: "Many people today, Chevalier, still know you best by the old and more widely renowned name of Casanova."

"I was not aware," said Lorenzi, with offensive gravity, "that the King of France had ennobled Signor Casanova."

"I was able to save the King that trouble," answered Casanova quietly. "I trust, Lieutenant Lorenzi, that you will be satisfied with an explanation to which the Burgomaster of Nuremberg offered no objection when I gave it to him in circumstances with which I need not weary the company." There was a moment of silent expectation. Casanova continued: "The alphabet is our common heritage. I chose a collocation of letters which pleased my taste, and ennobled myself without being indebted to any prince, who might perhaps have been disinclined to allow my claim. I style myself Casanova, Chevalier de Seingalt. I am indeed sorry, Lieutenant Lorenzi, if this name fails to meet with your approval."

"Seingalt! It is a splendid name," said the Abbate, repeating it several times, as if he were tasting it.

"There is not a man in the world," exclaimed Olivo, "who has a better right to name himself Chevalier than my distinguished friend Casanova!"

"As for you, Lorenzi," added the Marchese, "when your reputation has reached as far as that of Signor Casanova, Chevalier de Seingalt, we shall be willing enough, should you so desire, to give you also the title of Chevalier."

Casanova, somewhat nettled at not being allowed to fight his own battle, was about to resume the defence in person, when out of the dusk of the garden two elderly gentlemen, soberly habited, put in an appearance beside the table. Olivo greeted them with effusive cordiality, being delighted to turn the conversation and to put an end to a dispute that threatened to destroy the harmony of the evening. The newcomers were the brothers Ricardi. As Casanova had learned from Olivo, they were old bachelors. At one time members of the great world, they had been unfortunate in various undertakings. At length they had returned to their birthplace, the neighboring village, to lead a retired life in a tiny house they had rented. They were eccentric fellows, but quite harmless.

The Ricardis expressed their delight at renewing their acquaintance with the Chevalier, whom, they said, they had met in Paris a good many years ago.

Casanova could not recall the meeting.

"Perhaps it was in Madrid?" said the Ricardis.

"Maybe," replied Casanova, though he was absolutely certain that he had never seen either of them before.

The younger of the two was spokesman. The elder, who looked as if he might be ninety at least, accompanied his brother's words with incessant nods and grimaces. By now every one had left the table, and before this the children had disappeared. Lorenzi and the Marchesa were strolling in the dusk across the greensward. Marcolina and Amalia were in the hall, setting out the table for cards.

"What is the aim of all this?" said Casanova to himself, as he stood alone in the garden. "Do they imagine me to be rich? Are they on the lookout for plunder?"

These preparations, the ingratiating manners of the Marchese, the sedulous attentions of the Abbate, the appearance of the brothers Ricardi on the scene, were arousing his suspicions. Was it not possible that Lorenzi might be a party to the intrigue? Or Marcolina? Or even Amalia? For a moment it flashed through his mind that his enemies might be at work upon some scheme of the eleventh hour to make his return to Venice difficult or impossible. But a moment's reflection convinced him the notion was absurd—were it only because he no longer had any enemies. He was merely an old fellow in reduced circumstances. Who was likely to take any trouble to hinder his return to Venice? Glancing through the open window, he saw the company assembling round the table, where the cards lay ready, and the filled wine-glasses were standing. It seemed to him clear beyond all possibility of doubt that there was nothing afoot except an ordinary, innocent game of cards, in which the coming of a new player is always an agreeable change.

Marcolina passed him, and wished him good luck.

"Aren't you going to take a hand?" he said. "At least you will look on?"

"I have something else to do. Good night, Chevalier."

From the interior, voices called out into the night: "Lorenzi."—"Chevalier."—"We are waiting for you."

Casanova, standing in the darkness, could see that the Marchesa was leading Lorenzi away from the open greensward into the greater darkness under the trees. There she would fain have drawn him into her arms, but Lorenzi roughly tore himself away and strode towards the house. Meeting Casanova in the entry, he gave him precedence with mock politeness. Casanova accepted the precedence without a word of thanks.

The Marchese was the first banker. Olivo, the brothers Ricardi, and the Abbate staked such trifling amounts that to Casanova—even to-day when his whole worldly wealth consisted of no more than a few ducats—the game seemed ludicrous. All the more was this the case since the Marchese raked in his winnings and paid out his losses with a ceremonious air, as if he were handling enormous sums. Suddenly Lorenzi, who had hitherto taken no part in the game, staked a ducat, won, let the doubled stake stand; won again and again, and continued to have the same luck with but occasional interruptions. The other men, however, went on staking petty coins, and the two Ricardis in particular seemed quite annoyed if the Marchese failed to give them as much attention as he gave to Lieutenant Lorenzi. The two brothers played together upon the same hazard. Beads of perspiration formed upon the brow of the elder, who handled the cards. The younger, standing behind his brother, talked unceasingly, with the air of giving infallible counsel. When the silent brother won, the loquacious brother's eyes gleamed; but at a loss, he raised despairing eyes heavenward. The Abbate, impassive for the most part, occasionally enunciated some scrap of proverbial wisdom. For instance: "Luck and women cannot be constrained." Or, "The earth is round, and heaven is far away." At times he looked at Casanova with an air of sly encouragement, his eyes moving on from Casanova to rest upon Amalia where she sat beside her husband. It seemed as if his chief concern must be to bring the erstwhile lovers together once again.

As for Casanova, all he could think of was that Marcolina was in her room, undressing in leisurely fashion, and that if the window were open her white skin must be gleaming into the night. Seized with desire so intense as almost to put him beside himself, he moved to rise from his place by the Marchese and to leave the room. The Marchese, however, interpreting this movement as a resolve to take a hand in the game, said:

"At last! We were sure you would not be content to play the part of spectator, Chevalier."

The Marchese dealt him a card. Casanova staked all he had on his person, about ten ducats, which was nearly the whole of his entire wealth. Without counting the amount, he emptied his purse on the table, hoping to lose it at a single cast. That would be a sign of luck. He had not troubled to think precisely what sort of luck it would signify, whether his speedy return to Venice, or the desired sight of Marcolina's nudity. Ere he had made up his mind upon this point, the Marchese had lost the venture. Like Lorenzi, Casanova let the double stake lie; and just as in Lorenzi's case, fortune stood by him. The Marchese no longer troubled himself to deal to the others. The silent Ricardi rose somewhat mortified; the other Ricardi wrung his hands. Then the two withdrew, dumbfounded, to a corner of the room. The Abbate and Olivo took matters more phlegmatically. The former ate sweets and repeated his proverbial tags. The latter watched the turn of the cards with eager attention.

At length the Marchese had lost five hundred ducats to Casanova and Lorenzi. The Marchesa moved to depart, and looked significantly at the Lieutenant on her way out of the room. Amalia accompanied her guest. The Marchesa waddled in a manner that was extremely distasteful to Casanova. Amalia walked along beside her humbly and deprecatingly.

Now that the Marchese had lost all his ready cash, Casanova became banker, and, considerably to the Marchese's annoyance, he insisted that the others should return to the game. The brothers Ricardi eagerly accepted the invitation. The Abbate shook his head, saying he had had enough. Olivo played merely because he did not wish to be discourteous to his distinguished guest.

Lorenzi's luck held. When he had won four hundred ducats in all, he rose from the table, saying: "To-morrow I shall be happy to give you your revenge. But now, by your leave, I shall ride home."

"Home!" cried the Marchese with a scornful laugh—he had won back a few ducats by this time. "That is a strange way to phrase it!" He turned to the others: "The Lieutenant is staying with me. My wife has already driven home. I hope you'll have a pleasant time, Lorenzi!"

"You know perfectly well," rejoined Lorenzi imperturbably, "that I shall ride straight to Mantua, and not to your place, to which you were so good as to invite me yesterday."

"You can ride to bell for all I care!" said the other.

Lorenzi politely took his leave of the rest of the company, and, to Casanova's astonishment, departed without making any suitable retort to the Marchese.

Casanova went on with the game, still winning, so that the Marchese ere long was several hundred ducats in his debt. "What's the use of it all?" thought Casanova at first. But by degrees he was once more ensnared by the lure of the gaming table. "After all," he mused, "this is a lucky turn of fortune. I shall soon be a thousand to the good, perhaps even two thousand. The Marchese will not fail to pay his debt. It would be pleasant to take a modest competence with me to Venice. But why Venice? Who regains wealth, regains youth. Wealth is everything. At any rate, I shall now be able to buy her. Whom? The only woman I want.... She is standing naked at the window.... I am sure she is waiting there, expecting me to come.... She is standing at the window to drive me mad!"

All the same, with unruffled brow he continued dealing the cards, not only to the Marchese, but also to Olivo and to the brothers Ricardi. To the latter from time to time he pushed over a gold piece to which they had no claim, but which they accepted without comment. The noise of a trotting horse came from the road. "Lorenzi," thought Casanova. The hoofbeats echoed for a time from the garden wall, until sound and echo gradually died away.

At length Casanova's luck turned. The Marchese staked more and more boldly. By midnight Casanova was as poor as at the beginning; nay, poorer, for he had lost the few ducats with which he had made his first venture. Pushing the cards away, he stood up with a smile, saying: "Thank you, gentlemen, for a pleasant game."

Olivo stretched out both hands towards Casanova. "Dear friend, let us go on with the game..... You have a hundred and fifty ducats. Have you forgotten them? Not only a hundred and fifty ducats, but all that I have, everything, everything." His speech was thick, for he had been drinking throughout the evening.

Casanova signified his refusal with an exaggerated but courtly gesture. "Luck and women cannot be constrained," he said, bowing towards the Abbate, who nodded contentedly and clapped his hands.

"Till to-morrow, then, my dear Chevalier," said the Marchese. "We will join forces to win the money back from Lieutenant Lorenzi."

The brothers Ricardi insistently demanded that the game should continue. The Marchese, who was in a jovial mood, opened a bank for them. They staked the gold pieces which Casanova had allowed them to win. In a couple of minutes they had lost them all to the Marchese, who declined to go on playing unless they could produce cash. They wrung their hands. The elder began to cry like a child. The younger, to comfort his brother, kissed him on both cheeks. The Marchese enquired whether the carriage had returned, and the Abbate said he had heard it drive up half an hour earlier. Thereupon the Marchese offered the Abbate and the two Ricardis a lift, promising to set them down at their doors. All four left the house together.

When they had gone, Olivo took Casanova by the arm, and assured his guest repeatedly, with tears in his voice, that everything in the house was at Casanova's absolute disposal. They walked past Marcolina's window. Not merely was the window closed, but the iron grating had been fastened; within, the window was curtained. There had been times, thought Casanova, when all these precautions had been unavailing, or had been without significance. They reëntered the house. Olivo would not be dissuaded from accompanying the guest up the creaking staircase into the turret chamber. He embraced Casanova as he bade him good-night.

"To-morrow," he said, "you shall see the nunnery. But sleep as late as you please. We are not early risers here; anyhow we shall adapt the hours to your convenience. Good-night!" He closed the door quietly, but his heavy tread resounded through the house.

# CHAPTER IV.

The room in which Casanova was now left to his own devices was dimly lighted by two candles. His gaze roamed successively to the four windows, looking to the four quarters of heaven. The prospect was much the same from them all. The landscape had a bluish sheen. He saw broad plains with no more than trifling elevations, except to the northward where the mountains were faintly visible. A few isolated houses, farms, and larger buildings, could be made out. Among these latter was one which stood higher than the rest. Here there was still a light in one of the windows, and Casanova imagined it must be the Marchese's mansion.

The furniture of the room was simple. The double bed stood straight out into the room. The two candles were on a long table. There were a few chairs, and a chest of drawers bearing a gilt-framed mirror. Everything was in perfect order, and the valise had been unpacked. On the table, locked, lay the shabby portfolio containing Casanova's papers. There were also some books which he was using in his work; writing materials had been provided.

He did not feel sleepy. Taking his manuscript out of the portfolio, he reread what he had last written. Since he had broken off in the middle of a sentence, it was easy for him to continue. He took up the pen, wrote a phrase or two, then paused.

"To what purpose?" he demanded of himself, as if in a cruel flash of inner illumination. "Even if I knew that what I am writing, what I am going to write, would be considered incomparably fine; even if I could really succeed in annihilating Voltaire, and in making my renown greater than his—would I not gladly commit these papers to the flames could I but have Marcolina in my arms? For that boon, should I not be willing to vow never to set foot in Venice again, even though the Venetians should wish to escort me back to the city in triumph?"

"Venice!"..... He breathed the word once more. Its splendor captivated his imagination, and in a moment its old power over him had been restored. The city of his youth rose before his eyes, enshrined in all the charms of memory. His heart ached with yearning more intense than any that he could recall. To renounce the idea of returning home seemed to him the most incredible of the sacrifices which his destiny might demand. How could he go on living in this poor and faded world without the hope, without the certainty, that he was one day to see the beloved city again? After the years and decades of wanderings and adventures, after all the happiness and unhappiness he had experienced, after all the honor and all the shame, after so many triumphs and so many discomfitures—he must at length find a resting place, must at length find a home.

Was there any other home for him than Venice? Was there any good fortune reserved for him other than this, that he should have a home once more? It was long since in foreign regions he had been able to command enduring happiness. He could still at times grasp happiness, but for a moment only; he could no longer hold it fast. His power over his fellows, over women no less than over men, had vanished. Only where he evoked memories could his words, his voice, his glance, still conjure; apart from this, his presence was void of interest. His day was done!

He was willing to admit what he had hitherto been sedulous to conceal from himself, that even his literary labors, including the polemic against Voltaire upon which his last hopes reposed, would never secure any notable success. Here, likewise, he was too late. Had he in youth but had leisure and patience to devote himself seriously to the work of the pen, he was confident he could have ranked with the leading members of the profession of authorship, with the greatest imaginative writers and philosophers. He was as sure of this as he was sure that, granted more perseverance and foresight than he actually possessed, he could have risen to supreme eminence as financier or as diplomat.

But what availed his patience and his foresight, what became of all his plans in life, when the lure of a new love adventure summoned? Women, always women. For them he had again and again cast everything to the winds; sometimes for women who were refined, sometimes for women who were vulgar; for passionate women and for frigid women; for maidens and for harlots. All the honors and all the joys in the world had ever seemed cheap to him in comparison with a successful night upon a new love quest.

Did he regret what he had lost through his perpetual seeking and never or ever finding, through this earthly and superearthly flitting from craving to pleasure and from pleasure back to craving once more? No, he had no regrets. He had lived such a life as none other before him; and could he not still live it after his own fashion? Everywhere there remained women upon his path, even though they might no longer be quite so crazy about him as of old.

Amalia? He could have her for the asking, at this very hour, in her drunken husband's bed. The hostess in Mantua; was she not in love with him, fired with affection and jealousy as if he were a handsome lad? Perotti's mistress, pockmarked, but a woman with a fine figure? The very name of Casanova had intoxicated her with its aroma of a thousand conquests. Had she not implored him to grant her but a single night of love; and had he not spurned her as one who could still choose where he pleased?

But Marcolina—such as Marcolina were no longer at his disposal. Had such as Marcolina ever been at his disposal? Doubtless there were women of that kind. Perchance he had met more than one such woman before. Always, however, some more willing than she had been available, and he had never been the man to waste a day in vain sighing. Since not even Lorenzi had succeeded with Marcolina, since she had rejected the hand of this comely officer who was as handsome and as bold as he, Casanova, had been in youth, Marcolina might well prove to be that wonder of the world in the existence of which he had hitherto disbelieved—the virtuous woman.

At this juncture he laughed, so that the walls reëchoed. "The bungler, the greenhorn!" he exclaimed out loud, as so often in such self-communings. "He did not know how to make a good use of his opportunities. Or the Marchesa was hanging round his neck all the time. Or perhaps he took her as a next-best, when Marcolina, the philosopher, the woman of learning, proved unattainable!"

Suddenly a thought struck him. "To-morrow I will read her my polemic against Voltaire. I can think of no one else who would be a competent critic. I shall convince her. She will admire me. She will say: 'Excellent, Signor Casanova. Your style is that of a most brilliant old gentleman!' God!.... 'You have positively annihilated Voltaire, you brilliant senior!'"

He paced the chamber like a beast in a cage, hissing out the words in his anger. A terrible wrath possessed him, against Marcolina, against Voltaire, against himself, against the whole world. It was all he could do to restrain himself from roaring aloud in his rage. At length he threw himself upon the bed without undressing, and lay with eyes wide open, looking up at the joists among which spiders' webs were visible, glistening in the candlelight. Then, as often happened to him after playing cards late at night, pictures of cards chased one another swiftly through his brain, until he sank into a dreamless sleep.

His slumber was brief. When he awakened it was to a mysterious silence. The southern and the eastern windows of the turret chamber were open. Through them from the garden and the fields entered a complex of sweet odors. Gradually the silence was broken by the vague noises from near and from far which usually herald the dawn. Casanova could no longer lie quiet; a vigorous impulse towards movement gripped him, and lured him into the open. The song of the birds called to him; the cool breeze of early morning played upon his brow. Softly he opened the door and moved cautiously down the stairs. Cunning, from long experience, he was able to avoid making the old staircase creak. The lower flight, leading to the ground floor, was of stone. Through the hall, where half-emptied glasses were still standing on the table, he made his way into the garden. Since it was impossible to walk silently on the gravel, he promptly stepped on to the greensward, which now, in the early twilight, seemed an area of vast proportions. He slipped into the side alley, from which he could see Marcolina's window. It was closed, barred, and curtained, just as it had been overnight. Barely fifty paces from the house, Casanova seated himself upon a stone bench. He heard a cart roll by on the other side of the wall, and then everything was quiet again. A fine grey haze was floating over the greensward, giving it the aspect of a pond with fugitive outlines. Once again Casanova thought of that night long ago in the convent garden at Murano; he thought of another garden on another night; he hardly knew what memories he was recalling; perchance it was a composite reminiscence of a hundred nights, just as at times a hundred women whom he had loved would fuse in memory into one figure that loomed enigmatically before his questioning senses. After all, was not one night just like another? Was not one woman just like another? Especially when the affair was past and gone? The phrase, "past and gone," continued to hammer upon his temples, as if destined henceforth to become the pulse of his forlorn existence.

It seemed to him that something was rattling behind him along the wall. Or was it only an echo that he heard? Yes, the noise had really come from the house. Marcolina's window had suddenly been opened, the iron grating had been pushed back, the curtain drawn. A shadowy form was visible against the dark interior. Marcolina, clad in a white nightdress, was standing at the window, as if to breathe the fragrance of morning. In an instant, Casanova slipped behind the bench. Peeping over the top of it, through the foliage in the avenue, he watched Marcolina as if spellbound. She stood unthinking, it seemed, her gaze vaguely piercing the twilight. Not until several seconds had elapsed did she appear to collect herself, to grow fully awake and aware, directing her eyes slowly, now to right and now to left. Then she leaned forward, as if seeking for something on the gravel, and next she turned her head, from which her hair was hanging loosely, and looked up towards the windows in the upper story. Thereafter, she stood motionless for a while, supporting herself with a hand on either side of the window-frame as though she were fastened to an invisible cross. Now at length, suddenly illumined as it were from within, her features grew plain to Casanova's vision. A smile flitted across her face. Her arms fell to her sides; her lips moved strangely, as if whispering a prayer; once more she looked searchingly across the garden, then nodded almost imperceptibly, and at the instant someone who must hitherto have been crouching at her feet swung across the sill into the open. It was Lorenzi. He flew rather than walked across the gravel into the alley, which he crossed barely ten yards from Casanova, who held his breath as he lay behind the bench. Lorenzi, hastening on, made his way down a narrow strip of grass running along the wall, and disappeared from view. Casanova heard a door groan on its hinges—the very door doubtless through which he, Olivo, and the Marchese had reëntered the garden on the previous day—and then all was still. Marcolina had remained motionless. As soon as she knew that Lorenzi was safely away, she drew a deep breath, and closed grating and window. The curtain fell back into its place, and all was as it had been. Except for one thing; for now, as if there were no longer any reason for delay, day dawned over house and garden.

Casanova was still lying behind the bench, his arms outstretched before him. After a while he crept on all fours to the middle of the alley, and thence onward till he reached a place where he could not be seen from Marcolina's window or from any of the others. Rising to his feet with an aching back, he stretched body and limbs, and felt himself restored to his senses, as though re-transformed from a whipped hound into a human being—doomed to feel the chastisement, not as bodily pain, but as profound humiliation.

"Why," he asked himself, "did I not go to the window while it was still open? Why did I not leap over the sill? Could she have offered any resistance; would she have dared to do so; hypocrite, liar, strumpet?"

He continued to rail at her as though he had a right to do so, as though he had been her lover to whom she had plighted troth and whom she had betrayed. He swore to question her face to face; to denounce her before Olivo, Amalia, the Marchese, the Abbate, the servants, as nothing better than a lustful little whore. As if for practice, he recounted to himself in detail what he had just witnessed, delighting in the invention of incidents which would degrade her yet further. He would say that she had stood naked at the window; that she had permitted the unchaste caresses of her lover while the morning wind played upon them both.

After thus allaying the first vehemence of his anger, he turned to consider whether he might not make a better use of his present knowledge. Was she not in his power? Could he not now exact by threats the favors which she had not been willing to grant him for love? But this infamous design was speedily abandoned; not so much because Casanova realized its infamy, as because, even while the plan crossed his mind, he was aware of its futility. Why should Marcolina, accountable to no one but herself, be concerned at his threats? In the last resort she was astute enough, if needs must, to have him driven from the house as a slanderer and blackmailer. Even if, for one reason or another, she were willing to give herself to him in order to preserve the secret of her amours with Lorenzi (he was aware that he was speculating on something beyond the bounds of possibility), a pleasure thus extorted would become for him a nameless torment. Casanova knew himself to be one whose rapture in a love relationship was a thousandfold greater when conferring pleasure than when receiving it. Such a victory as he was contemplating would drive him to frenzy and despair.

Suddenly he found himself at the door in the garden wall. It was locked. Then Lorenzi had a master-key! But who, it now occurred to him to ask, had ridden the horse he had heard trotting away after Lorenzi had left the card table? A servant in waiting for the purpose, obviously.

Involuntarily Casanova smiled his approval. They were worthy of one another, these two, Marcolina and Lorenzi, the woman philosopher and the officer. A splendid career lay before them.

"Who will be Marcolina's next lover?" he thought questioningly. "The professor in Bologna in whose house she lives? Fool, fool! That is doubtless an old story. Who next? Olivo? The Abbate? Wherefore not? Or the serving-lad who stood gaping at the door yesterday when we drove up? She has given herself to all of them. I am sure of it. But Lorenzi does not know. I have stolen a march on him there."

Yet all the while he was inwardly convinced that Lorenzi was Marcolina's first lover. Nay, he even suspected that the previous night was the first on which she had given herself to Lorenzi. Nevertheless, as he made the circuit in the garden within the wall, he continued to indulge these spiteful, lascivious fantasies.

At length he reached the hall door, which he had left open. He must regain the turret chamber unseen and unheard. With all possible caution he crept upstairs, and sank into the armchair which stood in front of the table. The loose leaves of the manuscript seemed to have been awaiting his return. Involuntarily his eyes fell upon the sentence in the middle of which he had broken off. He read: "Voltaire will doubtless prove immortal. But this immortality will have been purchased at the price of his immortal part. Wit has consumed his heart just as doubt has consumed his soul, and therefore....."

At this moment the morning sun flooded the chamber with red light, so that the page in his hand glowed. As if vanquished, he laid it on the table beside the others. Suddenly aware that his lips were dry, he poured himself a glass of water from the carafe on the table; the drink was lukewarm and sweetish to the taste. Nauseated, he turned his head away from the glass, and found himself facing his image in the mirror upon the chest of drawers. A wan, aging countenance with dishevelled hair stared back at him. In a self-tormenting mood he allowed the corners of his mouth to droop as if he were playing the part of pantaloon on the stage; disarranged his hair yet more wildly; put out his tongue at his own image in the mirror; croaked a string of inane invectives against himself; and finally, like a naughty child, blew the leaves of his manuscript from the table on to the floor.

Then he began to rail against Marcolina again. He loaded her with obscene epithets. "Do you imagine," he hissed between his teeth, "that your pleasure will last? You will become fat and wrinkled and old just like the other women who were young when you were young. You will be an old woman with flaccid breasts; your hair will be dry and grizzled; you will be toothless, you will have a bad smell. Last of all you will die. Perhaps you will die while you are still quite young. You will become a mass of corruption, food for worms."

To wreak final vengeance upon her, he endeavored to picture her as dead. He saw her lying in an open coffin, wrapped in a white shroud. But he was unable to attach to her image any sign of decay, and her unearthly beauty aroused him to renewed frenzy. Through his closed eyelids he saw the coffin transform itself into a nuptial bed. Marcolina lay laughing there with lambent eyes. As if in mockery, with her small, white hands she unveiled her firm little breasts. But as he stretched forth his arms towards her, in the moment when he was about to clasp her in his passionate embrace, the vision faded.

# CHAPTER V.

Someone was knocking at the door. Casanova awoke from a heavy sleep to find Olivo standing before him.

"At your writing so early?"

Casanova promptly collected his wits. "It is my custom," he said, "to work the first thing in the morning. What time is it?"

"Eight o'clock," answered Olivo. "Breakfast is ready in the garden. We will start on our drive to the nunnery as early as you please, Chevalier. How the wind has blown your papers about!"

He stooped to pick up the fallen leaves. Casanova did not interfere. He had moved to the window, and was looking down upon the breakfast table which had been set on the greensward in the shade of the house. Amalia, Marcolina, and the three young girls, dressed in white, were at breakfast. They called up a good-morning. He had no eyes for anyone but Marcolina, who smiled at him frankly and in the friendliest fashion. In her lap was a plateful of early-ripe grapes, which she was eating deliberately.

Contempt, anger, and hatred vanished from Casanova's heart. All he knew was that he loved her. Made drunken by the very sight of her, he turned away from the window to find Olivo on hands and knees still assembling the scattered pages of manuscript from under the table and chest of drawers. "Don't trouble any further," he said to his host. "Leave me to myself for a moment while I get ready for the drive."

"No hurry," answered Olivo, rising, and brushing the dust from his knees. "We shall easily be home in time for dinner. We want to get back early, anyhow, for the Marchese would like us to begin cards soon after our meal. I suppose he wants to leave before sunset."

"It doesn't matter to me what time you begin cards," said Casanova, as he arranged his manuscript in the portfolio. "Whatever happens, I shall not take a hand in the game."

"Yes you will," explained Olivo with a decision foreign to his usual manner. Laying a roll of gold pieces on the table, he continued: "Thus do I pay my debt, Chevalier. A belated settlement, but it comes from a grateful heart." Casanova made a gesture of refusal.

"I insist," said Olivo. "If you do not take the money, you will wound us deeply. Besides, last night Amalia had a dream which will certainly induce you—but I will let her tell the story herself." He turned and left the room precipitately.

Casanova counted the money. Yes, there were one hundred and fifty gold pieces, the very sum that fifteen years earlier he had presented to the bridegroom, the bride, or the bride's mother—he had forgotten which.

"The best thing I could do," he mused, "would be to pack up the money, say farewell to Olivo and Amalia, and leave the place at once, if possible without seeing Marcolina again. Yet when was I ever guided by reason?—I wonder if news has reached Mantua from Venice? But my good hostess promised to forward without fail anything that might arrive."

The maid meanwhile had brought a large earthenware pitcher filled with water freshly drawn from the spring. Casanova sponged himself all over. Greatly refreshed, he dressed in his best suit, the one he had intended to wear the previous evening had there been time to change. Now, however, he was delighted that he would be able to appear before Marcolina better clad than on the previous day, to present himself in a new form as it were.

So he sauntered into the garden wearing a coat of grey satin richly embroidered and trimmed with Spanish lace; a yellow waistcoat; and knee-breeches of cherry-colored silk. His aspect was that of a man who was distinguished without being proud. An amiable smile played about his lips, and his eyes sparkled with the fire of inextinguishable youth. To his disappointment, he found no one but Olivo, who bade him be seated, and invited him to fall to upon the modest fare. Casanova's breakfast consisted of bread, butter, milk, and eggs, followed by peaches and grapes, which seemed to him the finest he had ever eaten. Now the three girls came running across the lawn. Casanova kissed them in turn, bestowing on the thirteen-year-old Teresina such caresses as the Abbate had been free with on the previous day. Her eyes gleamed in a way with which Casanova was familiar. He was convinced this meant something more to her than childish amusement.

Olivo was delighted to see how well the Chevalier got on with the girls. "Must you really leave us to-morrow morning?" he enquired tentatively. "This very evening," rejoined Casanova jovially. "You know, my dear Olivo, I must consider the wishes of the Venetian senators...."

"How have they earned the right to any such consideration from you?" broke in Olivo. "Let them wait. Stay here for another two days at least; or, better still, for a week."

Casanova slowly shook his head. He had seized Teresina's hands, and held her prisoner between his knees. She drew herself gently away, with a smile no longer that of a child. At this moment Amalia and Marcolina emerged from the house. Olivo besought them to second his invitation. But when neither found a word to say on the matter, Casanova's voice and expression assumed an unduly severe emphasis as he answered: "Quite out of the question."

On the way through the chestnut avenue to the road, Marcolina asked Casanova whether he had made satisfactory progress with the polemic. Olivo had told her that his guest had been at the writing-table since early morning.

Casanova was half inclined to make an answer that would have been malicious in its ambiguity, and would have startled his auditor without betraying himself. Reflecting, however, that premature advances could do his cause nothing but harm, he held his wit in leash, and civilly rejoined that he had been content to make a few emendations, the fruit of his conversation with her yesterday.

Now they all seated themselves in the lumbering carriage. Casanova sat opposite Marcolina, Olivo opposite Amalia. The vehicle was so roomy that, notwithstanding the inevitable joltings, the inmates were not unduly jostled one against the other. Casanova begged Amalia to tell him her dream. She smiled cordially, almost brightly, no longer displaying any trace of mortification or resentment.

"In my dream, Casanova, I saw you driving past a white building in a splendid carriage drawn by six chestnut horses. Or rather, the carriage pulled up in front of this building, and at first I did not know who was seated inside. Then you got out. You were wearing a magnificent white court dress embroidered with gold, so that your appearance was almost more resplendent than it is to-day." Her tone conveyed a spice of gentle mockery. "You were wearing, I am sure of it, the thin gold chain you are wearing to-day, and yet I had never seen it until this morning!" This chain, with the gold watch and gold snuff-box set with garnets (Casanova was fingering it as she spoke), were the only trinkets of value still left to him. "An old man, looking like a beggar, opened the carriage door. It was Lorenzi. As for you, Casanova, you were young, quite young, younger even than you seemed to me in those days." She said "in those days" quite unconcernedly, regardless of the fact that in the train of these words all her memories came attendant, winging their way like a flight of birds. "You bowed right and left, although there was not a soul within sight; then you entered the house. The door slammed to behind you. I did not know whether the storm had slammed it, or Lorenzi. So startling was the noise that the horses took fright and galloped away with the carriage. Then came a clamor from neighboring streets, as if people were trying to save themselves from being run over; but soon all was quiet again. Next I saw you at one of the windows. Now I knew it was a gaming-house. Once more you bowed in all directions, though the whole time there was no one to be seen. You looked over your shoulder, as if someone were standing behind you in the room; but I knew that no one was there. Now, of a sudden, I saw you at another window, in a higher story, where the same gestures were repeated. Then higher still, and higher, and yet higher, as if the building were piled story upon story, interminably. From each window in succession, you bowed towards the street, and then turned to speak to persons behind you—who were not really there at all. Lorenzi, meanwhile, kept on running up the stairs, flight after flight, but was never able to overtake you. He wanted you because you had forgotten to give him a gratuity....."

"What next?" enquired Casanova, when Amalia paused.

"There was a great deal more, but I have forgotten," said Amalia.

Casanova was disappointed. In such cases, whether he was relating a dream or giving an account of real incidents, it was his way to round off the narrative, attempting to convey a meaning. He remarked discontentedly: "How strangely everything is distorted in dreams. Fancy, that I should be wealthy; and that Lorenzi should be a beggar, and old!"

"As far as Lorenzi is concerned," interjected Olivo, "there is not much wealth about him. His father is fairly well off, but no one can say that of the son."

Casanova had no need to ask questions. He was speedily informed that it was through the Marchese that they had made the Lieutenant's acquaintance. The Marchese had brought Lorenzi to the house only a few weeks before. A man of the Chevalier's wide experience would hardly need prompting to enlighten him as to the nature of the young officer's relationship to the Marchesa. After all, if the husband had no objection, the affair was nobody else's business.

"I think, Olivo," said Casanova, "that you have allowed yourself to be convinced of the Marchese's complaisance too easily. Did you not notice his manner towards the young man, the mingling of contempt and ferocity? I should not like to wager that all will end well."

Marcolina remained impassive. She seemed to pay no attention to this talk about Lorenzi, but sat with unruffled countenance, and to all appearance quietly delighting in the landscape. The road led upwards by a gentle ascent zigzagging through groves of olives and holly trees. Now they reached a place where the horses had to go more slowly, and Casanova alighted to stroll beside the carriage. Marcolina talked of the lovely scenery round Bologna, and of the evening walks she was in the habit of taking with Professor Morgagni's daughter. She also mentioned that she was planning a journey to France next year, in order to make the personal acquaintance of Saugrenue, the celebrated mathematician at the university of Paris, with whom she had corresponded. "Perhaps," she said with a smile, "I may look in at Ferney on the way, in order to learn from Voltaire's own lips how he has been affected by the polemic of the Chevalier de Seingalt, his most formidable adversary."

Casanova was walking with a hand on the side of the carriage, close to Marcolina's arm. Her loose sleeve was touching his fingers. He answered quietly: "It matters less what M. Voltaire thinks about the matter than what posterity thinks. A final decision upon the merits of the controversy must be left to the next generation."

"Do you really think," said Marcolina earnestly, "that final decisions can be reached in questions of this character?"

"I am surprised that you should ask such a thing, Marcolina. Though your philosophic views, and (if the term be appropriate) your religious views, seem to me by no means irrefutable, at least they must be firmly established in your soul—if you believe that there is a soul."

Marcolina, ignoring the personal animus in Casanova's words, sat looking skyward over the tree-crests, and tranquilly rejoined: "Ofttimes, and especially on a day like this"—to Casanova, knowing what he knew, the words conveyed the thrill of reverence in the newly awakened heart of a woman—"I feel as if all that people speak of as philosophy and religion were no more than playing with words. A sport nobler perhaps than others, nevertheless more unmeaning than them all. Infinity and eternity will never be within the grasp of our understanding. Our path leads from birth to death. What else is left for us than to live a life accordant with the law that each of us bears within—or a life of rebellion against that law? For rebellion and submissiveness both issue from God."

Olivo looked at his niece with timid admiration, then turned to contemplate Casanova with some anxiety. Casanova was in search of a rejoinder which should convince Marcolina that she was in one breath affirming and denying God, or should prove to her that she was proclaiming God and the Devil to be the same. He realized, however, that he had nothing but empty words to set against her feelings, and to-day words did not come to him readily. His expression showed him to be somewhat at a loss, and apparently reminded Amalia of the confused menaces he had uttered on the previous day. So she hastened to remark: "Marcolina is deeply religious all the same, I can assure you, Chevalier."

Marcolina smiled.

"We are all religious in our several ways," said Casanova civilly.

Now came a turn in the road, and the nunnery was in sight. The slender tops of cypresses showed above the encircling wall. At the sound of the approaching carriage, the great doors had swung open. The porter, an old man with a flowing white beard, bowed gravely and gave them admittance. Through the cloisters, between the columns of which they caught glimpses of an overgrown garden, they advanced towards the main building, from whose unadorned, grey, and prison-like exterior an unpleasantly cool air was wafted. Olivo pulled the bellrope; the answering sound was high-pitched, and died away in a moment. A veiled nun silently appeared, and ushered the guests into the spacious parlor. It contained merely a few plain wooden chairs, and the back was cut off by a heavy iron grating, beyond which nothing could be seen but a vague darkness.

With bitterness in his heart, Casanova recalled the adventure which still seemed to him the most wonderful of all his experiences. It had begun in just such surroundings as the present. Before his eyes loomed the forms of the two inmates of the Murano convent who had been friends in their love for him. In conjunction they had bestowed upon him hours of incomparable sweetness. When Olivo, in a whisper, began to speak of the strict discipline imposed upon this sisterhood—once they were professed, the nuns must never appear unveiled before a man, and they were vowed to perpetual silence—a smile flitted across Casanova's face.

The Abbess suddenly emerged from the gloom, and was standing in their midst. In silence she saluted her guests, and with an exaggerated reverence of her veiled head acknowledged Casanova's expressions of gratitude for the admission of himself, a stranger. But when Marcolina wished to kiss her hand, the Abbess gathered the girl in her arms. Then, with a wave of the hand inviting them to follow, she led the way through a small room into a cloister surrounding a quadrangular flower-garden. In contrast to the outer garden, which had run wild, this inner garden was tended with especial care. The flower-beds, brilliant in the sunshine, showed a wonderful play of variegated colors. The warm odors were almost intoxicating. One, intermingled with the rest, aroused no responsive echo in Casanova's memory. Puzzled, he was about to say a word on the subject to Marcolina, when he perceived that the enigmatic, stimulating fragrance emanated from herself. She had removed her shawl from her shoulders and was carrying it over her arm. From the opening of her gown came a perfume at once kindred to that of the thousand flowers of the garden, and yet unique.

The Abbess, still without a word, conducted the visitors between the flower-beds upon narrow, winding paths which traversed the garden like a lovely labyrinth. The graceful ease of her gait showed that she was enjoying the chance of showing others the motley splendors of her garden. As if she had determined to make her guests giddy, she moved on faster and ever faster like the leader of a lively folk-dance. Then, quite suddenly, so that Casanova seemed to awaken from a confusing dream, they all found themselves in the parlor once more. On the other side of the grating, dim figures were moving. It was impossible to distinguish whether, behind the thick bars, three or five or twenty veiled women were flitting to and fro like startled ghosts. Indeed, none but Casanova, with eyes preternaturally acute to pierce the darkness, could discern that they were human outlines at all.

The Abbess attended her guests to the door, mutely gave them a sign of farewell, and vanished before they had found time to express their thanks for her courtesy.

Suddenly, just as they were about to leave the parlor, a woman's voice near the grating breathed the word "Casanova." Nothing but his name, in a tone that seemed to him quite unfamiliar. From whom came this breach of a sacred vow? Was it a woman he had once loved, or a woman he had never seen before? Did the syllables convey the ecstasy of an unexpected reencounter, or the pain of something irrecoverably lost; or did it convey the lamentation that an ardent wish of earlier days had been so late and so fruitlessly fulfilled? Casanova could not tell. All that he knew was that his name, which had so often voiced the whispers of tender affection, the stammerings of passion, the acclamations of happiness, had today for the first time pierced his heart with the full resonance of love. But, for this very reason, to probe the matter curiously would have seemed to him ignoble and foolish. The door closed behind the party, shutting in a secret which he was never to unriddle. Were it not that the expression on each face had shown timidly and fugitively that the call to Casanova had reached the ears of all, each might have fancied himself or herself a prey to illusion. No one uttered a word as they walked through the cloisters to the great doors. Casanova brought up the rear, with bowed head, as if on the occasion of some profoundly affecting farewell.

The porter was waiting. He received his alms. The visitors stepped into the carriage, and started on the homeward road. Olivo seemed perplexed; Amalia was distrait. Marcolina, however, was quite unmoved. Too pointedly, in Casanova's estimation, she attempted to engage Amalia in a discussion of household affairs, a topic upon which Olivo was compelled to come to his wife's assistance. Casanova soon joined in the discussion, which turned upon matters relating to kitchen and cellar. An expert on these topics, he saw no reason why he should hide his light under a bushel, and he seized the opportunity of giving a fresh proof of versatility. Thereupon, Amalia roused herself from her brown study. After their recent experience—at once incredible and haunting—to all, and especially to Casanova, there was a certain comfort derivable from an extremely commonplace atmosphere of mundane life. When the carriage reached home, where an inviting odor of roast meat and cooking vegetables assailed their nostrils, Casanova was in the midst of an appetizing description of a Polish pasty, a description to which even Marcolina attended with a flattering air of domesticity.

# CHAPTER VI.

In a strangely tranquillized, almost happy mood, which was a surprise to himself, Casanova sat at table with the others, and paid court to Marcolina in the sportive manner which might seem appropriate from a distinguished elderly gentleman towards a well-bred young woman of the burgher class. She accepted his attentions gracefully, in the spirit in which they appeared to be offered. He found it difficult to believe that his demure neighbor was the same Marcolina from whose bedroom window he had seen a young officer emerge, a man who had obviously held her in his arms but a few moments earlier. It was equally difficult for him to realize how this tender girl, who was fond of romping on the grass with other children, could conduct a learned correspondence with Saugrenue, the renowned mathematician of Paris. Yet simultaneously he derided himself for the inertness of his imagination. Had he not learned a thousand times that in the souls of all persons who are truly alive, discrepant elements, nay, apparently hostile elements, may coexist in perfect harmony? He himself, who shortly before had been so profoundly moved, had been desperate, had been ready for evil deeds, was now so gentle, so kindly, in so merry a mood, that Olivo's little daughters were shaking their sides with laughter. Nevertheless, as was usual with him after strong excitement, his appetite was positively ferocious, and this served to warn him that order was not yet fully restored in his soul.

With the last course, the maid brought in a despatch which had just arrived for the Chevalier by special messenger from Mantua. Olivo noticed that Casanova grew pale. He told the servant to provide the messenger with refreshment, then turned to his guest.

"Pray don't stand upon ceremony, Chevalier. Read your letter."

"If you will excuse me," answered Casanova. He went to the window and opened the missive with simulated indifference. It was from Signor Bragadino, an old friend of the family and a confirmed bachelor, over eighty years of age, and for the last decade a member of the Supreme Council. He had shown more interest than other patrons in pressing Casanova's suit. The letter was beautifully written, although the characters were a little shaky. It was as follows:

> "My dear Casanova:
>
> "I am delighted, at length, to be able to send you news which will, I hope, be substantially accordant with your wishes. The Supreme Council, at its last sitting, which took place yesterday evening, did not merely express its willingness to permit your return to Venice. It went further. The Council desires that your advent

should be as speedy as possible, since there is an intention to turn to immediate account the active gratitude which you have foreshadowed in so many of your letters.

"Since Venice has been deprived for so long of the advantage of your presence, you may perhaps be unaware, my dear Casanova, that quite recently the internal affairs of our beloved native city have taken a rather unfavorable trend both politically and morally. Secret societies have come into existence, directed against the constitution of the Venetian state, and even, it would seem, aiming at its forcible overthrow. As might be expected, the members of these societies, persons whom it would not be too harsh to denominate conspirators, are chiefly drawn from certain free-thinking, irreligious, and lawless circles. Not to speak of what goes on in private, we learn that in the public squares and in coffee houses, the most outrageous, the most treasonable conversations, take place. But only in exceptional instances has it been possible to catch the guilty in the act, or to secure definite proof against the offenders. A few admissions have been enforced by the rack, but these confessions have proved so untrustworthy that several members of the Council are of opinion that for the future it would be better to abstain from methods of investigation which are not only cruel but are apt to lead us astray. Of course there is no lack of individuals well-affected towards public order and devoted to the welfare of the state, individuals who would be delighted to place their services at the disposal of the government; but most of them are so well known as stalwart supporters of the existing constitution that when they are present people are chary in their utterances and are most unlikely to give vent to treasonable expressions.

"At yesterday's sitting, one of the senators, whom I will not name, expressed the opinion that a man who had the reputation of being without moral principle and who was furthermore regarded as a freethinker—in short, Casanova, such a man as yourself—if recalled to Venice would not fail to secure prompt and sympathetic welcome in the very circles which the government regards with such well-grounded suspicion. If he played his cards well, such a man would soon inspire the most absolute confidence.

"In my opinion, irresistibly, and as if by the force of a law of nature, there would gravitate around your person the very elements which the Supreme Council, in its indefatigable zeal for the state, is most eager to render harmless and to punish in an exemplary manner. For your part, my dear Casanova, you would give us an acceptable proof of your patriotic zeal, and would furnish in addition an infallible sign of your complete conversion from all those tendencies for which, during your imprisonment in The

Leads, you had to atone by punishment which, though severe, was not, as you now see for yourself (if we are to believe your epistolary assurances), altogether unmerited. I mean, should you be prepared, immediately on your return home, to act in the way previously suggested, to seek acquaintance with the elements sufficiently specified above, to introduce yourself to them in the friendliest fashion as one who cherishes the same tendencies, and to furnish the Senate with accurate and full reports of everything which might seem to you suspicious or worthy of note.

"For these services the authorities would offer you, to begin with, a salary of two hundred and fifty lire per month, apart from special payments in cases of exceptional importance. I need hardly say that you would receive in addition, without too close a scrutiny of the items, an allowance for such expenses as you might incur in the discharge of your duties (I refer, for instance, to the treating of this individual or of that, little gifts made to women, and so on).

"I do not attempt to conceal from myself that you may have to fight down certain scruples before you will feel inclined to fulfil our wishes. Permit me, however, as your old and sincere friend (who was himself young once), to remind you that it can never be regarded as dishonorable for a man to perform any services that may be essential for the safety of his beloved fatherland—even if, to a shallow-minded and unpatriotic citizen, such services might seem to be of an unworthy character. Let me add, Casanova, that your knowledge of human nature will certainly enable you to draw a distinction between levity and criminality, to differentiate the jester from the heretic. Thus it will be within your power, in appropriate cases, to temper justice with mercy, and to deliver up to punishment those only who, in your honest opinion, may deserve it.

"Above all I would ask you to consider that, should you reject the gracious proposal of the Supreme Council, the fulfilment of your dearest wish—your return to Venice—is likely to be postponed for a long and I fear for an indefinite period; and that I myself, if I may allude to the matter, as an old man of eighty-one, should be compelled in all human probability to renounce the pleasing prospect of ever seeing you again in this life.

"Since, for obvious reasons, your appointment will be of a confidential and not of a public nature, I beg you to address to me personally your reply, for which I make myself responsible, and which I wish to present to the Council at its next sitting a week hence. Act with all convenient speed, for, as I have previously explained, we are daily receiving offers from thoroughly trustworthy persons who, from patriotic motives, voluntarily place themselves at the disposal of the Supreme Council. Nevertheless, there is hardly one among them who can compare with you, my dear Casanova, in respect of experience or intelligence. If, in addition to all the arguments I have adduced, you take my personal feelings into account, I find it difficult to doubt that you will gladly respond to the call which now reaches you from so exalted and so friendly a source.

"Till then, receive the assurances of my undying friendship.

"BRAGADINO."

"Postscript. Immediately upon receipt of your acceptance, it will be a pleasure to me to send you a remittance of two hundred lire through the banking firm of Valori in Mantua. The sum is to defray the cost of your journey.

"B."

Long after Casanova had finished reading the letter, he stood holding the paper so as to conceal the deathly pallor of his countenance. From the dining-table came a continuous noise, the rattle of plates and the clinking of glasses; but conversation had entirely ceased. At length Amalia ventured to say: "The food is getting cold, Chevalier; won't you go on with your meal?"

"You must excuse me," replied Casanova, letting his face be seen once more, for by now, owing to his extraordinary self-control, he had regained outward composure. "I have just received the best possible news from Venice, and I must reply instantly. With your leave, I will go to my room."

"Suit yourself, Chevalier," said Olivo. "But do not forget that our card party begins in an hour."

In the turret chamber Casanova sank into a chair. A chill sweat broke out over his body; he shivered as if in the cold stage of a fever; he was seized with such nausea that he felt as if he were about to choke. For a time he was unable to think clearly, and he could do no more than devote his energies to the task of self-restraint without quite knowing why he did so. But there was no one in the house upon whom he could vent his fury; and he could not fail to realize the utter absurdity of a half-formed idea that Marcolina must be in some way contributory to the intolerable shame which had been put upon him.

As soon as he was in some degree once more master of himself, his first thought was to take revenge upon the scoundrels who had believed that he could be hired as a police spy. He would return to Venice in disguise, and would exert all his cunning to compass the death of these wretches—or at least of whomever it was that had conceived the despicable design.

Was Bragadino the prime culprit? Why not? An old man so lost to all sense of shame that he had dared to write such a letter to Casanova; a dotard who could actually believe that Casanova, whom he had personally known, would set his hand to this ignominious task. He no longer knew Casanova! Nor did anyone know him, in Venice or elsewhere. But people should learn to know him once more.

It was true that he was no longer young enough or handsome enough to seduce an honest girl. Nor did he now possess the skill and the agility requisite for an escape from prison, or for gymnastic feats upon the roof-tops. But in spite of his age, he was cleverer than anyone else! Once back in Venice, he could do anything he pleased. The first step, the essential step, was to get back. Perhaps it would not be necessary to kill anyone. There were other kinds of revenge, grimmer, more devilish, than a commonplace murder. If he were to feign acceptance of the Council's proposal, it would be the easiest thing in the world to compass the destruction of those whom he wished to destroy, instead of bringing about the ruin of those whom the authorities had in mind, and who were doubtless the finest fellows among all the inhabitants of Venice! Monstrous! Because they were the enemies of this infamous government, because they were reputed heretics, were they to languish in The Leads where he had languished twenty-five years ago, or were they to perish under the executioner's axe? He detested the government a hundred times more than they did, and with better reason. He had been a lifelong heretic; was a heretic to-day, upon sincerer conviction than them all. What a queer comedy he had been playing of late years—simply from tedium and disgust. He to believe in God? What sort of a God was it who was gracious only to the young, and left the old in the lurch? A God who, when the fancy took him, became a devil; who transformed wealth into poverty, fortune into misfortune, happiness into despair. "You play with us—and we are to worship you? To doubt your existence is the only resource left open to us if we are not to blaspheme you! You do not exist; for if you did exist, I should curse you!"

Shaking his clenched fists heavenward, he rose to his feet. Involuntarily, a detested name rose to his lips. Voltaire! Yes, now he was in the right mood to finish his polemic against the sage of Ferney. To finish it? No, now was the time to begin it. A new one! A different one! One in which the ridiculous old fool should be shown up as he deserved: for his pusillanimity, his half-heartedness, his subservience. He an unbeliever? A man of whom the latest news was that he was on excellent terms with the priests, that he visited church, and on feast days actually went to confession! He a heretic? He was a chatterbox, a boastful coward, nothing more! But the day of reckoning was at hand, and soon there would be nothing left of the great philosopher but a quill-driving buffoon.

What airs he had given himself, this worthy M. Voltaire! "My dear M. Casanova, I am really vexed with you. What concern have I with the works of Merlin? It is your fault that I have wasted four hours over such nonsense."

All a matter of taste, excellent M. Voltaire! People will continue to read Merlin long after *La Pucelle* has been forgotten. Possibly they will continue to prize my sonnets, the sonnets you returned to me with a shameless smile, and without saying a word about them. But these are trifles. Do not let us spoil a great opportunity because of our sensitiveness as authors. We are concerned with philosophy—with God! We shall cross swords, M. Voltaire, unless you die before I have a chance to deal with you.

He was already in the mind to begin his new polemic, when it occurred to him that the messenger was waiting for an answer. He hastily indited a letter to the old duffer Bragadino, a letter full of hypocritical humility and simulated delight. With joy and gratitude he accepted the pardon of the Council. He would expect the remittance by return of post, so that with all possible speed he might present himself before his patrons, and above all before the honored old family friend, Bragadino.

When he was in the act of sealing the letter, someone knocked gently at the door. At the word, Olivo's eldest daughter, the thirteen-year-old Teresina, entered, to tell him that the whole company was assembled below, and that the Chevalier was impatiently awaited at the card table. Her eyes gleamed strangely; her cheeks were flushed; her thick, black hair lay loose upon her temples; her little mouth was half open.

"Have you been drinking wine, Teresina?" asked Casanova striding towards her.

"Yes. How did you know?" She blushed deeper, and in her embarrassment she moistened her lips with her tongue.

Casanova seized her by the shoulders, and, breathing in her face, drew her to the bed. She looked at him with great helpless eyes in which the light was now extinguished. But when she opened her mouth as if to scream, Casanova's aspect was so menacing that she was almost paralyzed with fear, and let him do whatever he pleased.

He kissed her with a tender fierceness, whispering: "You must not tell the Abbate anything about this, Teresina, not even in confession. Some day, when you have a lover or a husband, there is no reason why he should know anything about it. You should always keep your own counsel. Never tell the truth to your father, your mother, or your sisters, that it may be well with you on earth. Mark my words." As he spoke thus blasphemously, Teresina seemed to regard his utterance as a pious admonition, for she seized his hand and kissed it reverently as if it had been a priest's.

He laughed. "Come," he said, "come, little wife, we will walk arm in arm into the room downstairs!"

She seemed a little coy at first, but smiled with genuine gratification.

It was high time for them to go down, for they met Olivo coming up. He was flushed and wore a frown, so that Casanova promptly inferred that the Marchese or the Abbate had roused his suspicions by some coarse jest concerning Teresina's prolonged absence. His brow cleared when he beheld Casanova on the threshold, standing arm in arm with the girl as if in sport.

"I'm sorry to have kept you all waiting, Olivo," said Casanova. "I had to finish my letter." He held the missive out to Olivo in proof of his words.

"Take it," said Olivo to Teresina, smoothing her rumpled hair. "Hand it to the messenger."

"Here are two gold pieces for the man," added Casanova. "He must bestir himself, so that the letter may leave Mantua for Venice to-day. And ask him to tell my hostess at the inn that I shall return this evening."

"This evening?" exclaimed Olivo. "Impossible!"

"Oh, well, we'll see," observed Casanova affably. "Here, Teresina, take this, a gold piece for yourself." When Olivo demurred, Casanova added: "Put it in your moneybox, Teresina. That letter is worth any amount of gold pieces!"

Teresina tripped away, and Casanova nodded to himself contentedly. In days gone by he had possessed the girl's mother and grandmother also, and he thought it a particularly good joke that he was paying the little wench for her favors under the very eyes of her father.

# CHAPTER VII.

When Casanova entered the hall with Olivo, cards had already begun. He acknowledged with serene dignity the effusive greeting of the company, and took his place opposite the Marchese, who was banker. The windows into the garden were open. Casanova heard voices outside; Marcolina and Amalia strolled by, glanced into the room for a moment, and then disappeared.

While the Marchese was dealing, Lorenzi turned to Casanova with ceremonious politeness, saying: "My compliments, Chevalier. You were better informed than I. My regiment is under orders to march tomorrow afternoon."

The Marchese looked surprised. "Why did you not tell us sooner, Lorenzi?"

"The matter did not seem of such supreme importance."

"It is of no great importance to me," said the Marchese. "But don't you think it is of considerable importance to my wife?" He laughed raucously. "As a matter of fact, I have some interest in the matter myself. You won four hundred ducats from me yesterday, and there is not much time left in which to win them back."

"The Lieutenant won money from us too," said the younger Ricardi. The elder, silent as usual, looked over his shoulder at his brother, who stood behind the elder's chair as on the previous day.

"Luck and women....." began the Abbate.

The Marchese finished the sentence for him: ".....cannot be constrained."

Lorenzi carelessly scattered his gold on the table. "There you are. I will stake it all upon a single card, if you like, Marchese, so that you need not wait for your money."

Casanova suddenly became aware of a feeling of compassion for Lorenzi, a feeling he was puzzled to account for. But he believed himself to be endowed with second-sight, and he had a premonition that the Lieutenant would fall in his first encounter.

The Marchese did not accept the suggestion of high stakes, nor did Lorenzi insist. They resumed the game, therefore, much as on the previous night, everyone taking a hand at first, and only moderate sums being ventured. A quarter of an hour later, however, the stakes began to rise, and ere long Lorenzi had lost his four hundred ducats to the Marchese.

Casanova had no constancy either in luck or ill-luck. He won, lost, and won again, in an almost ludicrously regular alternation.

Lorenzi drew a breath of relief when his last gold piece had gone the way of the others. Rising from the table, he said: "I thank you, gentlemen. This," he hesitated for a moment, "this will prove to have been my last game for a long time in your hospitable house. If you will allow me, Signor Olivo, I will take leave of the ladies before riding into town. I must reach Mantua ere nightfall in order to make preparations for to-morrow."

"Shameless liar," thought Casanova. "You will return here to-night, to Marcolina's arms!" Rage flamed up in him anew.

"What!" exclaimed the Marchese maliciously. "The evening will not come for hours. Is the game to stop so early? If you like, Lorenzi, my coachman shall drive home with a message to the Marchesa to let her know that you will be late."

"I am going to ride to Mantua," rejoined Lorenzi impatiently. The Marchese, ignoring this statement, went on: "There is still plenty of time. Put up some of your own money, if it be but a single gold piece." He dealt Lorenzi a card.

"I have not a single gold piece left," said Lorenzi wearily.

"Really?"

"Not one," asserted Lorenzi, as if tired of the whole matter.

"Never mind," said the Marchese, with a sudden assumption of amiability which was far from congenial. "I will trust you as far as ten ducats goes, or even for a larger sum if needs must."

"All right, a ducat, then," said Lorenzi, taking up the card dealt to him.

The Marchese won. Lorenzi went on with the game, as if this were now a matter of course, and was soon in the Marchese's debt to the amount of one hundred ducats.

At this stage Casanova became banker, and had even better luck than the Marchese. There remained only three players. To-day the brothers Ricardi stood aside without complaint. Olivo and the Abbate were merely interested onlookers.

No one uttered a syllable. Only the cards spoke, and they spoke in unmistakable terms. By the hazard of fortune all the cash found its way to Casanova. In an hour he had won two thousand ducats; he had won them from Lorenzi, though they came out of the pockets of the Marchese, who at length sat there without a soldo.

Casanova offered him whatever gold pieces he might need. The Marchese shook his head. "Thanks," he said, "I have had enough. The game is over as far as I am concerned."

From the garden came the laughing voices of the girls. Casanova heard Teresina's voice in particular, but he was sitting with his back to the window and did not turn round. He tried once more to persuade the Marchese to resume the game—for the sake of Lorenzi, though he hardly knew what moved him. The Marchese refused with a yet more decisive headshake.

Lorenzi rose, saying: "I shall have the honor, Signor Marchese, of handing the amount I owe you to you personally, before noon to-morrow."

The Marchese laughed drily. "I am curious to know how you will manage that, Lieutenant Lorenzi. There is not a soul, in Mantua or elsewhere, who would lend you as much as ten ducats, not to speak of two thousand, especially to-day. For to-morrow you will be on the march, and who can tell whether you will ever return?"

"I give you my word of honor, Signor Marchese, that you shall have the money at eight o'clock to-morrow morning."

"Your word of honor," said the Marchese, "is not worth a single ducat to me, let alone two thousand."

The others held their breath. Lorenzi, apparently unmoved, merely answered: "You will give me satisfaction, Signor Marchese."

"With pleasure, Signor Lieutenant," rejoined the Marchese, "as soon as you have paid your debt."

Olivo, who was profoundly distressed, here intervened, stammering slightly: "I stand surety for the amount, Signor Marchese. Unfortunately I have not sufficient ready money on the spot; but there is the house, the estate....." He closed the sentence with an awkward wave of the hand.

"I refuse to accept your surety, for your own sake," said the Marchese. "You would lose your money."

Casanova saw that all eyes were turned towards the gold that lay on the table before him. "What if I were to stand surety for Lorenzi," he thought. "What if I were to pay the debt for him? The Marchese could not refuse my offer. I almost think I ought to do it. It was the Marchese's money."

But he said not a word. He felt that a plan was taking shape in his mind, and that above all he needed time in which he might become clear as to its details.

"You shall have the money this evening, before nightfall," said Lorenzi. "I shall be in Mantua in an hour."

"Your horse may break its neck," replied the Marchese. "You too; intentionally, perhaps."

"Anyhow," said the Abbate indignantly, "the Lieutenant cannot get the money here by magic."

The two Ricardis laughed; but instantly restrained their mirth.

Olivo once more addressed the Marchese. "It is plain that you must grant Lieutenant Lorenzi leave to depart."

"Yes, if he gives me a pledge," exclaimed the Marchese with flashing eyes, as if this idea gave him peculiar delight.

"That seems rather a good plan," said Casanova, a little absent-mindedly, for his scheme was ripening.

Lorenzi drew a ring from his finger and flicked it across the table.

The Marchese took it up, saying: "That is good for a thousand."

"What about this one?" Lorenzi threw down another ring in front of the Marchese.

The latter nodded, saying: "That is good for the same amount."

"Are you satisfied now, Signor Marchese?" enquired Lorenzi, moving as if to go.

"I am satisfied," answered the Marchese, with an evil chuckle; "all the more, seeing that the rings are stolen."

Lorenzi turned sharply, clenching his fist as if about to strike the Marchese. Olivo and the Abbate seized Lorenzi's arm.

"I know both the stones, though they have been reset," said the Marchese without moving from his place. "Look, gentlemen, the emerald is slightly flawed, or it would be worth ten times the amount. The ruby is flawless, but it is not a large one. Both the stones come from a set of jewels which I once gave my wife. And, since it is quite impossible for me to suppose that the Marchesa had them reset in rings for Lieutenant Lorenzi, it is obvious that they have been stolen—that the whole set has been stolen. Well, well, the pledge suffices, Signor Lieutenant, for the nonce."

"Lorenzi!" cried Olivo, "we all give you our word that no one shall ever hear a syllable from us about what has just happened."

"And whatever Signor Lorenzi may have done," said Casanova, "you, Signor Marchese, are the greater rascal of the two."

"I hope so," replied the Marchese. "When anyone is as old as we are, Chevalier de Seingalt, assuredly he should not need lessons in rascality. Good-evening, gentlemen."

He rose to his feet. No one responded to his farewell, and he went out.

For a space the silence was so intense, that once again the girls' laughter was heard from the garden, now seeming unduly loud.

Who would have ventured to utter the word that was searing Lorenzi's soul, as he stood at the table with his arm still raised? Casanova, the only one of the company who had remained seated, derived an involuntary artistic pleasure from the contemplation of this fine, threatening gesture, meaningless now, but seemingly petrified, as if the young man had been transformed into a statue.

At length Olivo turned to him with a soothing air; the Ricardis, too, drew near; and the Abbate appeared to be working himself up for a speech. But a sort of shiver passed over Lorenzi's frame. Automatically but insistently he silently indicated his rejection of any offers at intervention. Then, with a polite inclination of the head, he quietly left the room.

Casanova, who had meanwhile wrapped up the money in a silken kerchief, instantly followed. Without looking at the others' faces, he could feel that they were convinced it was his instant intention to do what they had all the while been expecting, namely, to place his winnings at Lorenzi's disposal.

# CHAPTER VIII.

Casanova overtook Lorenzi in the chestnut avenue. Speaking lightly, he said: "May I have the pleasure of accompanying you on your walk, Lieutenant Lorenzi?"

Lorenzi, without looking at him, answered in an arrogant tone which seemed hardly in keeping with his situation: "As you please, Chevalier; but I am afraid you will not find me an amusing companion."

"Perhaps, Lieutenant, you will on the other hand find me an entertaining companion. If you have no objection, let us take the path through the vineyard, where our conversation will be undisturbed."

They turned aside from the high-road into the narrow footway running beside the garden wall, along which Casanova had walked with Olivo on the previous day.

"You are right in supposing," began Casanova, "that I have it in mind to offer you the sum of money which you owe to the Marchese. Not as a loan. That, if you will excuse my saying so, seems to me rather too risky a venture. I could let you have it as a slight return for a service which I think you may be able to do me."

"Go on," said Lorenzi coldly.

"Before I say any more," answered Casanova, in a similar tone, "I must make a condition upon your acceptance of which the continuance of this conversation depends."

"Name your condition."

"Give me your word of honor that you will listen to me without interruption, even though what I have to say may arouse your displeasure or your wrath. When you have heard me to the end, it will rest entirely with yourself whether you accept a proposal which, I am well aware, is of an extremely unusual nature. But I want you to answer it with a simple Yes or No. Whatever the issue, no one is to hear a word concerning what passes at this interview between two men of honor, who are perhaps no better than they should be."

"I am ready to listen to your proposal."

"You accept my condition?"

"I will not interrupt you."

"And you will answer nothing beyond Yes or No?"

"Nothing beyond Yes or No."

"Very well," said Casanova. They walked slowly up the hill, between the vine stocks, in the sultry heat of the late afternoon. Casanova began to speak: "We shall perhaps understand one another best if we discuss the matter logically. It is obvious that you have absolutely no chance of obtaining the money you owe the Marchese within the prescribed time. There can be no doubt that he has made up his mind to ruin you should you fail to pay. Since he knows more of you than he actually disclosed to us to-day"—Casanova was venturing beyond the limits of his own knowledge, but he loved to take these little risks when following up a path decided on in advance—"you are absolutely in the power of the old ruffian, and your fate as an officer and a gentleman would be sealed. There you have one side of the question. On the other hand, you will be saved as soon as you have paid your debt, and as soon as you get back those rings—however you may have come by them. This will mean the recovery of an existence which is otherwise practically closed. Since you are young, handsome, and bold, it will mean the recovery of an existence which offers splendor, happiness, and renown. This appears to me a most attractive prospect; especially seeing that the only alternative is an inglorious, nay, a shameful ruin; for such a prospect, I should be willing to sacrifice a prejudice which I had never really possessed. I am well aware, Lorenzi," he added quickly, as if expecting contradiction and desiring to forestall it, "I am well aware, that you have no more prejudices than I have or ever had. What I am going to ask of you is merely what I should in your place under like circumstances be willing to do, without a moment's hesitation. Indeed, I have never hesitated, at the call of destiny or as the outcome of caprice, to commit a rascality, or rather, that to which fools give such a name. Like you, Lorenzi, I have ever been ready to hazard my life for less than nothing, and to call it quits. I am ready to do so now, if my proposal prove inacceptable. We are made of the same stuff, you and I; we are brothers in spirit; we may therefore disclose our souls to one another without false shame, proud in our nakedness. Here are my two thousand ducats. Call them yours, if you enable me to spend to-night in your place with Marcolina.—Let us not stand still, if you please, Lorenzi. Let us continue our walk." They walked through the fields, beneath the fruit trees, between which the vines, heavy with grape-clusters, were trellised. Casanova went on without a pause: "Don't answer me yet, Lorenzi, for I have not finished. My request would naturally be, if not monstrous, at least preposterous, if it were your intention to make Marcolina your wife, or if Marcolina's own hopes or wishes turned in this direction. But just as last night was your first night spent in love together"—he uttered this guess as if he had absolute knowledge of the fact—"so also was the ensuing night predestined, according to all human calculation, according to your own expectations and Marcolina's, to be your last night together for a long period and probably for ever. I am absolutely convinced that Marcolina herself, in order to save her lover from certain destruction, and simply upon his wish, would be perfectly willing to give this one night to his savior. For she, too, is a philosopher, and is therefore just as free from prejudices as we are. Nevertheless, certain as I am that she would meet the test, I am far from intending that it should be imposed upon her. To possess a woman outwardly passive but inwardly resistant, would be far from satisfying my desires, least of all in the present case. I wish, not merely as a lover, but also as one beloved, to taste a rapture which I should be prepared to pay for with my life. Understand this clearly, Lorenzi. For the reason I have explained, Marcolina must not for an instant suspect that I am the man whom she is clasping to her sweet bosom; she must be firmly convinced that you are in her arms. It is your part to pave the way for this deception; mine to maintain it. You will not have much difficulty in making her understand that you will have to leave her before dawn. Nor need you be at a loss for a pretext as to the necessity for perfectly mute caresses when you return at night, as you will promise to return. To avert all danger of discovery at the last moment, I shall, when the time comes for me to leave, act as if I heard a suspicious noise outside the window. Seizing my cloak,—or rather yours, which you must of course lend me for the occasion—I shall vanish through the window, never to return. For, of course, I shall take my leave this evening. But half-way back to Mantua, telling the coachman that I have forgotten some important papers, I shall return here on foot. Entering the garden by the side door (you must give me the master-key), I shall creep to Marcolina's window, which must be opened for me at midnight. I shall have taken off my clothes in the carriage, even to my shoes and stockings, and shall wear only your cloak, so that when I take to flight nothing will be left to betray either you or me. The cloak and the two thousand ducats will be at your disposal at five o'clock to-morrow morning in the inn at Mantua, so that you may deliver over the money to the Marchese even before the appointed hour. I pledge my solemn oath to fulfil my side of the bargain. I have finished."

Suddenly he stood still. The sun was near to setting. A gentle breeze made the yellow ears rustle; the tower of Olivo's house glowed red in the evening light. Lorenzi, too, halted. His pale face was motionless, as he gazed into vacancy over Casanova's shoulder. His arms hung limp by his sides, whereas Casanova's hand, ready for any emergency, rested as if by chance upon the hilt of his sword. A few seconds elapsed, and Lorenzi was still silent. He seemed immersed in tranquil thought, but Casanova remained on the alert, holding the kerchief with the ducats in his left hand, but keeping the right upon his sword-hilt. He spoke once more.

"You have honorably fulfilled my conditions. I know that it has not been easy. For even though we may be free from prejudices, the atmosphere in which we live is so full of them that we cannot wholly escape their influence. And just as you, Lorenzi, during the last quarter of an hour, have more than once been on the point of seizing me by the throat; so I, I must confess, played for a time with the idea of giving you the two thousand ducats as to my friend. Rarely, Lorenzi, have I been so strangely drawn to anyone as I was to you from the first. But had I yielded to this generous impulse, the next moment I should have regretted it bitterly. In like manner you, Lorenzi, in the moment before you blow your brains out, would desperately regret having been such a fool as to throw away a thousand nights of love with new and ever new women for one single night of love which neither night nor day was to follow."

Lorenzi remained mute. His silence continued for many minutes, until Casanova began to ask himself how long his patience was to be tried. He was on the point of departing with a curt salutation, and of thus indicating that he understood his proposition to have been rejected, when Lorenzi, without a word slowly moved his right hand backwards into the tail-pocket of his coat. Casanova, ever on his guard, instantly stepped back a pace, and was ready to duck. Lorenzi handed him the key of the garden door.

Casanova's movement, which had certainly betokened fear, brought to Lorenzi's lips the flicker of a contemptuous smile. Casanova was able to repress all sign of his rising anger, for he knew that had he given way to it he might have ruined his design. Taking the key with a nod, he merely said: "No doubt that means Yes. In an hour from now—an hour will suffice for your understanding with Marcolina—I shall expect you in the turret chamber. There, in exchange for your cloak, I shall have the pleasure of handing you the two thousand gold pieces without further delay. First of all, as a token of confidence; and secondly because I really do not know what I should do with the money during the night."

They parted without further formality. Lorenzi returned to the house by the path along which they had both come. Casanova made his way to the village by a different route. At the inn there, by paying a considerable sum as earnest money, he was able to arrange for a carriage to await him at ten o'clock that evening for the drive from Olivo's house into Mantua.

# CHAPTER IX.

Returning to the house, Casanova disposed of his gold in a safe corner of the turret chamber. Thence he descended to the garden, where a spectacle awaited him, not in itself remarkable, but one which touched him strangely in his present mood. Upon a bench at the edge of the greensward Olivo was sitting beside Amalia, his arm round her waist. Reclining at their feet were the three girls, tired out by the afternoon's play. Maria, the youngest, had her head in her mother's lap, and seemed to be asleep; Nanetta lay at full length on the grass with her head pillowed on her arm; Teresina was leaning against her father's knee, and he was stroking her hair. As Casanova drew near, Teresina greeted him, not with the look of lascivious understanding which he had involuntarily expected, but with a frank smile of childlike confidence, as if what had passed between them only a few hours before had been nothing more than some trivial pastime. Olivo's face lighted up in friendly fashion, and Amalia nodded a cordial greeting. It was plain to Casanova that they were receiving him as one who had just performed a generous deed, but who would prefer, from a sense of refinement, that no allusion should be made to the matter.

"Are you really determined to leave us tomorrow, Chevalier?" enquired Olivo.

"Not to-morrow," answered Casanova, "but, as I told you, this very evening."

Olivo would fain have renewed his protests, but Casanova shrugged, saying in a tone of regret: "Unfortunately, my letter from Venice leaves me no option. The summons sent to me is so honorable in every respect that to delay my return home would be an unpardonable affront to my distinguished patrons." He asked his host and hostess to excuse him for a brief space. He would go to his room, make all ready for departure, and would then be able to enjoy the last hours of his stay undisturbed in his dear friends' company.

Disregarding further entreaties, he went to the turret chamber, and first of all changed his attire, since the simpler suit must suffice for the journey. He then packed his valise, and listened for Lorenzi's footsteps with an interest which grew keener from moment to moment. Before the time was up, Lorenzi, knocking once at the door, entered, wearing a dark blue riding-cloak. Without a word, he slipped the cloak from his shoulders and let it fall to the floor, where it lay between the two men, a shapeless mass of cloth. Casanova withdrew his kerchief filled with the gold pieces from beneath the bolster, and emptied the money on the table. He counted the coins under Lorenzi's eyes—a process which was soon over, for many of the gold pieces were worth several ducats each. Putting the stipulated sum into two purses, he handed these to Lorenzi. This left about a hundred ducats for himself. Lorenzi stuffed the purses into his tail-pockets, and was about to leave, still silent.

"Wait a moment, Lorenzi," said Casanova. "Our paths in life may cross once again. If so let us meet as friends. We have made a bargain like many another bargain; let us cry quits."

Casanova held out his hand. Lorenzi would not take it. He spoke for the first time. "I cannot recall that anything was said about this in our agreement." Turning on his heel he left the room. "Do we stand so strictly upon the letter, my friend?" thought Casanova. "It behooves me all the more to see to it that I am not duped in the end." In truth, he had given no serious thought to this possibility. He knew from personal experience that such men as Lorenzi have their own peculiar code of honor, a code which cannot be written in formal propositions, but which they can be relied upon to observe.

He packed Lorenzi's cloak in the top of the valise. Having stowed away upon his person the remaining gold pieces, he took a final glance round the room which he was never likely to revisit. Then with sword and hat, ready for the journey, he made his way to the hall, where he found Olivo, Amalia, and the children already seated at table. At the same instant, Marcolina entered by the garden door. The coincidence was interpreted by Casanova as a propitious sign. She answered his salutation with a frank inclination of the head.

Supper was now served. The conversation dragged a little at first, as if all were oppressed by the thought of the imminent leave-taking. Amalia seemed busied with her girls, concerned to see that they were not helped to too much or too little. Olivo, somewhat irrelevantly, began to speak of a trifling lawsuit he had just won against a neighboring landowner. Next he referred to a business journey to Mantua and Cremona, which he would shortly have to undertake. Casanova expressed the hope that ere long he would be able to entertain his friend in Venice, a city which, by a strange chance, Olivo had never visited. Amalia had seen the place of wonder as a child. She could not recall the journey thither, but could only remember having seen an old man wrapped in a scarlet cloak, disembarking from a long black boat. He had stumbled and had fallen prone.

"Have you never been to Venice either?" asked Casanova of Marcolina, who was seated facing him, so that she could see over his shoulder into the deep gloom of the garden. She shook her head. Casanova mused: "If I could but show you the city in which I passed my youth! Had you but been young with me!" Another thought, as foolish as both of these, crossed his mind: "Even now, if I could but take you there with me."

While thus thinking, at the same time, with the ease of manner peculiar to him in moments of great excitement, he began to speak of his native city. At first his language was cool; he used an artist's touch, as if painting a picture. Warming up by degrees, he entered into details of personal history, so that of a sudden his own figure appeared in the centre of the canvas, filling it with life. He spoke of his mother, the celebrated actress, for whom her admirer Goldoni had written his admirable comedy, *La Pupilla*. Next he recounted the unhappy days spent in Dr.

Gozzi's boarding school. Then he spoke of his childish passion for the gardener's little daughter, who had subsequently run away with a lackey; of his first sermon as a young abbate, after which he found in the offertory bag, in addition to the usual collection, a number of love letters; of his doings as a fiddler in the orchestra of the San Samueli Theatre; of the pranks which he and his companions had played in the alleys, taverns, dancing halls, and gaming-houses of Venice—sometimes masked and sometimes unmasked. In telling the story of these riotous escapades, he was careful to avoid the use of any offensive epithet. He phrased his narrative in choice imaginative language, as if paying due regard to the presence of the young girls, who, like their elders, including Marcolina, listened with rapt attention. The hour grew late, and Amalia sent her daughters to bed. They all kissed Casanova a tender good-night, Teresina behaving exactly like her sisters. He made them promise that they would soon come with their father and mother to visit him in Venice. When they had gone, he spoke with less restraint, but continued to avoid any unsuitable innuendo or display of vanity. His audience might have imagined themselves listening to the story of a Parsifal rather than to that of a Casanova, the dangerous seducer and half-savage adventurer.

He told them of the fair Unknown who had travelled with him for weeks disguised as a man in officer's uniform, and one morning had suddenly disappeared from his side; of the daughter of the gentleman cobbler in Madrid who, in the intervals between their embraces, had studiously endeavored to make a good Catholic of him; of Lia, the lovely Jewess of Turin, who had a better seat on horseback than any princess; of Manon Balletti, sweet and innocent, the only woman he had almost married; of the singer whom he had hissed in Warsaw because of her bad performance, whereupon he had had to fight a duel with her lover, General Branitzky, and had been compelled to flee the city; of the wicked woman Charpillon, who had made such an abject fool of him in London; of the night when he crossed the lagoons to Murano on the way to his adored nun, the night when he nearly lost his life in a storm; of Croce the gamester, who, after losing a fortune at Spa, had taken a tearful farewell of Casanova upon the high-road, and had set off on his way to St. Petersburg, just as he was, wearing silk stockings and a coat of apple-green satin, and carrying nothing but a walking cane.

He told of actresses, singers, dressmakers, countesses, dancers, chambermaids; of gamblers, officers, princes, envoys, financiers, musicians, and adventurers. So carried away was he by the rediscovered charm of his own past, so completely did the triumph of these splendid though irrecoverable experiences eclipse the consciousness of the shadows that encompassed his present, that he was on the point of telling the story of a pale but pretty girl who in a twilit church at Mantua had confided her love troubles to him—absolutely forgetting that this same girl, sixteen years older, now sat at the table before him as the wife of his friend Olivo—when the maid came in to say that the carriage was waiting. Instantly, with his incomparable talent for doing the right thing, Casanova rose to bid adieu. He again pressed Olivo, who was too much affected to speak, to bring wife and children to visit him in Venice. Having embraced his friend, he approached Amalia with intent to embrace her also, but she held out her hand and he kissed it affectionately.

When he turned to Marcolina, she said: "You ought to write down everything you told us this evening, Chevalier, and a great deal more, just as you have penned the story of your flight from The Leads."

"Do you really mean that, Marcolina?" he enquired, with the shyness of a young author.

She smiled with gentle mockery, saying: "I fancy such a book might prove far more entertaining than your polemic against Voltaire."

"Very likely," he thought. "Perhaps I may follow your advice some day. If so, you, Marcolina, shall be the theme of the last chapter."

This notion, and still more the thought that the last chapter was to be lived through that very night, made his face light up so strangely that Marcolina, who had given him her hand in farewell, drew it away again before he could stoop to kiss it. Without betraying either disappointment or anger, Casanova turned to depart, after signifying, with one of those simple gestures of which he was a master, his desire that no one, not even Olivo, should follow him.

He strode rapidly through the chestnut avenue, handed a gold piece to the maid who had brought his valise to the carriage, took his seat and drove away.

The sky was overcast. In the village, lamps were still burning in some of the cottages; but by the time the carriage regained the open road, the only light piercing the darkness was supplied by the yellow rays of the lantern dangling from the shaft. Casanova opened the valise, took out Lorenzi's cloak, flung it over his shoulders, and under this cover rapidly undressed. He packed the discarded clothing, together with shoes and stockings, in the valise, and wrapped himself in the cloak. Then he called to the coachman:

"Stop, we must drive back!"

The coachman turned heavily in his seat.

"I have left some of my papers in the house. Don't you understand? We must drive back."

When the coachman, a surly, thin greybeard, still hesitated, Casanova said: "Of course I will pay you extra for your trouble. Here you are!" He pressed a gold piece into the man's hand.

The coachman nodded, muttered something, gave his horse a needless cut with the whip, and turned the carriage round. When they drove back through the village, all the houses were dark. A little farther on, the coachman was about to turn into the by-road leading up the gentle ascent to Olivo's house.

"Halt!" cried Casanova. "We won't drive any nearer, lest we should wake them all up. Wait for me here at the corner. I shall be back in a minute or two. If I should happen to keep you longer, you shall have a ducat for every hour!"

The man by his nod seemed to show he understood what was afoot.

Casanova descended and made quickly past the closed door and along the wall to the corner. Here began the path leading through the vineyards. It still led along the wall. Having walked it twice by daylight, Casanova had no difficulty in the dark. Half way up the hill came a second angle in the wall. Here he had again to turn to the right, across soft meadow-land, and in the pitchy night had to feel along the wall until he found the garden door. At length his fingers recognized the change from smooth stone to rough wood, and he could easily make out the framework of the narrow door. He unlocked it, entered the garden, and made all fast again behind him.

Across the greensward he could now discern house and tower. They seemed incredibly far off and yet incredibly large. He stood where he was for a while, looking around. What to other eyes would have been impenetrable darkness, was to him no more than deep twilight. The gravel path being painful to his bare feet, he walked upon the greensward, where, moreover, his footfall made no sound. So light was his tread that he felt as if soaring.

"Has my mood changed," he thought, "since those days when, as a man of thirty, I sought such adventures? Do I not now, as then, feel all the ardors of desire and all the sap of youth course through my veins? Am I not, as of old, Casanova? Being Casanova, why should I be subject, as others are subject, to the pitiful law which is called age!"

Growing bolder, he asked himself: "Why am I creeping in disguise to Marcolina? Is not Casanova a better man than Lorenzi, even though he be thirty years older? Is not she the one woman who would have understood the incomprehensible? Was it needful to commit this lesser rascality, and to mislead another man into the commission of a greater rascality? Should I not, with a little patience, have reached the same goal? Lorenzi would in any case have gone to-morrow, whilst I should have remained. Five days, three days, and she would have given herself to me, knowing me to be Casanova."

He stood close to the wall of the house beneath Marcolina's window, which was still closed. His thoughts ran on: "Is it too late? I could come back to-morrow or the next day. Could begin the work of seduction—in honorable fashion, so to speak. To-night would be but a foretaste of the future. Marcolina must not learn that I have been here to-day—or not until much later."

# CHAPTER X.

Marcolina's window was still closed. There was no sign from within. It wanted a few minutes to midnight. Should he make his presence known in any way? By tapping gently at the window? Since nothing of this sort had been arranged, it might arouse Marcolina's suspicions. Better wait. It could not be much longer. The thought that she might instantly recognize him, might detect the fraud before he had achieved his purpose, crossed his mind—not for the first time, yet as a passing fancy, as a remote possibility which it was logical to take into account, but not anything to be seriously dreaded.

A ludicrous adventure now recurred to his mind. Twenty years ago he had spent a night with a middle-aged ugly vixen in Soleure, when he had imagined himself to be possessing a beautiful young woman whom he adored. He recalled how next day, in a shameless letter, she had derided him for the mistake that she had so greatly desired him to make and that she had compassed with such infamous cunning. He shuddered at the thought. It was the last thing he would have wished to think of just now, and he drove the detestable image from his mind.

It must be midnight! How long was he to stand shivering there? Waiting in vain, perhaps? Cheated, after all? Two thousand ducats for nothing. Lorenzi behind the curtain, mocking at the fool outside!

Involuntarily he gripped the hilt of the sword he carried beneath the cloak, pressed to his naked body. After all, with a fellow like Lorenzi one must be prepared for any tricks.

At that instant he heard a gentle rattling, and knew it was made by the grating of Marcolina's window in opening. Then both wings of the window were drawn back, though the curtain still veiled the interior. Casanova remained motionless for a few seconds more, until the curtain was pulled aside by an unseen hand. Taking this as a sign, he swung himself over the sill into the room, and promptly closed window and grating behind him. The curtain had fallen across his shoulders, so that he had to push his way beneath it. Now he would have been in absolute darkness had there not been shining from the depths of the distance, incredibly far away, as if awakened by his own gaze, the faintest possible illumination to show him the way. No more than three paces forward, and eager arms enfolded him. Letting the sword slip from his hand, the cloak from his shoulders, he gave himself up to his bliss.

From Marcolina's sigh of surrender, from the tears of happiness which he kissed from her cheeks, from the ever-renewed warmth with which she received his caresses, he felt sure that she shared his rapture; and to him this rapture seemed more intense than he had ever experienced, seemed to possess a new and strange quality. Pleasure became worship; passion was transfused with an intense consciousness. Here at last was the reality which he had often falsely imagined himself to be on the point of attaining, and which had always eluded his grasp. He held in his arms a woman upon whom he could squander himself, with whom he could feel himself inexhaustible; the woman upon whose breast the moment of ultimate self-abandonment and of renewed desire seemed to coalesce into a single instant of hitherto unimagined spiritual ecstasy. Were not life and death, time and eternity, one upon these lips? Was he not a god? Were not youth and age merely a fable; visions of men's fancy? Were not home and exile, splendor and misery, renown and oblivion, senseless distinctions, fit only for the use of the uneasy, the lonely, the frustrate; had not the words become unmeaning to one who was Casanova, and who had found Marcolina?

More contemptible, more absurd, as the minutes passed, seemed to him the prospect of keeping the resolution which he had made when still pusillanimous, of acting on the determination to flee out of this night of miracle dumbly, unrecognized, like a thief. With the infallible conviction that he must be the bringer of delight even as he was the receiver of delight, he felt prepared for the venture of disclosing his name, even though he knew all the time that he would thus play for a great stake, the loss of which would involve the loss of his very existence. He was still shrouded in impenetrable darkness, and until the first glimmer of dawn made its way through the thick curtain, he could postpone a confession upon whose favorable acceptance by Marcolina his fate, nay his life, depended.

Besides, was not this mute, passionately sweet association the very thing to bind Marcolina to him more firmly with each kiss that they enjoyed? Would not the ineffable bliss of this night transmute into truth what had been conceived in falsehood? His duped mistress, woman of women, had she not already an inkling that it was not Lorenzi, the stripling, but Casanova, the man, with whom she was mingling in these divine ardors?

He began to deem it possible that he might be spared the so greatly desired and yet so intensely dreaded moment of revelation. He fancied that Marcolina, thrilling, entranced, transfigured, would spontaneously whisper his name. Then, when she had forgiven him, he would take her with him that very hour. Together they would leave the house in the grey dawn; together they would seek the carriage that was waiting at the turn of the road; together they would drive away. She would be his for evermore. This would be the crown of his life; that at an age when others were doomed to a sad senility, he, by the overwhelming might of his unconquerable personality, would have won for himself the youngest, the most beautiful, the most gifted of women.

For this woman was his as no woman had ever been before. He glided with her through mysterious, narrow canals, between palaces in whose shadows he was once more at home, under high-arched bridges which blurred figures were swiftly crossing. Many of the wayfarers glanced down for a moment over the parapet, and vanished ere their faces could be discerned.

Now the gondola drew alongside. A marble stairway led up to the stately mansion of Senator Bragadino. It was the only palace holding festival. Masked guests were ascending and descending. Many of them paused with inquisitive glances; but who could recognize Casanova and Marcolina in their dominoes?

He entered the hall with her. Here was a great company playing for high stakes. All the senators, Bragadino among them, were seated round the table in their purple robes. As Casanova came through the door, they whispered his name as if terror-stricken, for the flashing of his eyes behind the mask had disclosed his identity. He did not sit down; he did not take any cards, and yet he joined in the game. He won. He won all the gold on the table, and this did not suffice. The senators had to give him notes of hand. They lost their possessions, their palaces, their purple robes; they were beggars; they crawled round him clad in rags, kissing his hands.

Nearby, in a hall with crimson hangings, there was music and dancing. Casanova wished to dance with Marcolina, but she had vanished. Once again the senators in their purple robes were seated at the table; but now Casanova knew that the hazards at stake were not those of a game of cards; he knew that the destinies of accused persons, some criminal and some innocent, hung in the balance.

What had become of Marcolina? Had he not been holding her by the hand all the time? He rushed down the staircase. The gondola was waiting. On, on, through the maze of canals. Of course the gondolier knew where Marcolina was; but why was he, too, masked? That had not been the custom of old in Venice. Casanova wished to question him, but was afraid. Does a man become so cowardly when he grows old?

Onward, ever onward. How huge Venice had grown during these five-and-twenty years! At length the houses came to an end; the canal opened out; they were passing between islands; there stood the walls of the Murano nunnery, to which Marcolina had fled.

There was no gondola now; he had to swim; how delightful! It was true that in Venice the children were playing with his gold pieces. But what was money to him? The water was now warm, now cold; it dripped from his clothing as he climbed over the wall.

"Where is Marcolina?" he enquired in the parlor, in loud, challenging tones such as only a prince would dare to use.

"I will summon her," said the Lady Abbess, and sank into the ground.

Casanova wandered about; he had wings; he fluttered to and fro along the gratings, fluttered like a bat. "If I had only known sooner that I can fly," he thought. "I will teach Marcolina."

Behind the gratings, the figures of women were moving hither and thither. They were nuns—and yet they were all wearing secular dress. He knew it, though he could not really see them. He knew who they were. Henriette the Unknown; Corticelli and Cristina, the dancers; the bride; Dubois the Beautiful; the accurst vixen of Soleure; Manon Balletti; a hundred others—but never Marcolina!

"You have betrayed me," he cried to the gondolier, who was waiting for him beneath. Never had he hated anyone as he hated this gondolier, and he swore to take an exquisite revenge.

But how foolish he had been to seek Marcolina in the Murano nunnery when she had gone to visit Voltaire. It was fortunate that he could fly, since he had no money left with which to pay for a carriage.

He swam away. But he was no longer enjoying himself. The water grew colder and colder; he was drifting out into the open sea, far from Murano, far from Venice, and there was no ship within sight; his heavy gold-embroidered garments were dragging him down; he tried to strip them off, but it was impossible, for he was holding his manuscript, the manuscript he had to give to M. Voltaire. The water was pouring into his mouth and nose; deadly fear seized him; he clutched at impalpable things; there was a rattling in his throat; he screamed; and with a great effort he opened his eyes.

Between the curtain and the window-frame the dawn was making its way through in a narrow strip of light. Marcolina, in her white nightdress and with hands crossed upon her bosom, was standing at the foot of the bed contemplating Casanova with unutterable horror. Her glance instantly recalled him to his senses. Involuntarily he stretched out his arms towards her with a gesture of appeal. Marcolina, as if rejecting this appeal, waved him away with her left hand, while with the right she continued to grasp her raiment convulsively. Casanova sat up, his eyes riveted upon her. Neither was able to look away from the other. His expression was one of rage and shame; hers was one of shame and disgust. Casanova knew how she saw him, for he saw himself figured in imagination, just as he had seen himself yesterday in the bedroom mirror. A yellow, evil face, deeply lined, with thin lips and staring eyes—a face three times worse than that of yesterday, because of the excesses of the night, the ghastly dream of the morning, and the terrible awakening. And what he read in Marcolina's countenance was not what he would a thousand times rather have read there; it was not thief, libertine, villain. He read only something which crushed him to earth more ignominiously than could any terms of abuse; he read the word which to him was the most dreadful of all words, since it passed a final judgment upon him—old man.

Had it been within his power to annihilate himself by a spell, he would have done so, that he might be spared from having to creep out of the bed and display himself to Marcolina in his nakedness, which must appear to her more loathsome than the sight of some loathsome beast.

But Marcolina, as if gradually collecting herself, and manifestly in order to give him the opportunity which was indispensable, turned her face to the wall. He seized the moment to get out of bed, to raise the cloak from the floor, and to wrap himself in it. He was quick, too, to make sure of his sword. Now, when he conceived himself to have at least escaped the worst contumely of all, that of ludicrousness, he began to wonder whether it would not be possible to throw another light upon this affair in which he cut so pitiful a figure. He was an adept in the use of language. Could he not somehow or other, by a few well-chosen words, give matters a favorable turn?

From the nature of the circumstances, it was evidently impossible for Marcolina to doubt that Lorenzi had sold her to Casanova. Yet however intensely she might hate her wretched lover at that moment, Casanova felt that he himself, the cowardly thief, must seem a thousand times more hateful.

Perhaps another course offered better promise of satisfaction. He might degrade Marcolina by mockery and lascivious phrases, full of innuendo. But this spiteful idea could not be sustained in face of the aspect she had now assumed. Her expression of horror had gradually been transformed into one of infinite sadness, as if it had been not Marcolina's womanhood alone which had been desecrated by Casanova, but as if during the night that had just closed a nameless and inexpiable offence had been committed by cunning against trust, by lust against love, by age against youth. Beneath this gaze which, to Casanova's extremest torment, reawakened for a brief space all that was still good in him, he turned away. Without looking round at Marcolina, he went to the window, drew the curtain aside, opened casement and grating, cast a glance round the garden which still seemed to slumber in the twilight, and swung himself across the sill into the open.

Aware of the possibility that someone in the house might already be awake and might spy him from a window, he avoided the greensward and sought cover in the shaded alley. Passing through the door in the wall, he had hardly closed it behind him, when someone blocked his path. "The gondolier!" was his first idea. For now he suddenly realized that the gondolier in his dream had been Lorenzi. The young officer stood before him. His silver-braided scarlet tunic glowed in the morning light.

"What a splendid uniform," was the thought that crossed Casanova's confused, weary brain. "It looks quite new. I am sure it has not been paid for." These trivial reflections helped him to the full recovery of his wits; and as soon as he realized the situation, his mind was filled with gladness. Drawing himself up proudly, and grasping the hilt of his sword firmly beneath the cloak, he said in a tone of the utmost amiability: "Does it not seem to you, Lieutenant Lorenzi, that this notion of yours has come a thought too late?"

"By no means," answered Lorenzi, looking handsomer than any man Casanova had ever seen before. "Only one of us two shall leave the place alive."

"What a hurry you are in, Lorenzi," said Casanova in an almost tender tone. "Cannot the affair rest until we reach Mantua? I shall be delighted to give you a lift in my carriage, which is waiting at the turn of the road. There is a great deal to be said for observing the forms in these matters, especially in such a case as ours."

"No forms are needed. You or I, Casanova, at this very hour." He drew his sword.

Casanova shrugged. "Just as you please, Lorenzi. But you might at least remember that I shall be reluctantly compelled to appear in a very inappropriate costume." He threw open the cloak and stood there nude, playing with the sword in his hand.

Hate welled up in Lorenzi's eyes. "You shall not be at any disadvantage," he said, and began to strip with all possible speed.

Casanova turned away, and for the moment wrapped himself in his cloak once more, for though the sun was already piercing the morning mists, the air was chill. Long shadows lay across the fields, cast by the sparse trees on the hill-top. For an instant Casanova wondered whether someone might not come down the path. Doubtless it was used only by Olivo and the members of his household. It occurred to Casanova that these were perhaps the last minutes of his life, and he was amazed at his own calmness.

"M. Voltaire is a lucky fellow," came as a passing thought. But in truth he had no interest in Voltaire, and he would have been glad at this supreme moment to have been able to call up pleasanter images than that of the old author's vulturine physiognomy. How strange it was that no birds were piping in the trees over the wall. A change of weather must be imminent. But what did the weather matter to him? He would rather think of Marcolina, of the ecstasy he had enjoyed in her arms, and for which he was now to pay dear. Dear? Cheap enough! A few years of an old man's life in penury and obscurity. What was there left for him to do in the world? To poison Bragadino? Was it worth the trouble? Nothing was worth the trouble. How few trees there were on the hill! He began to count them. "Five... seven... ten.—Have I nothing better to do?"

"I am ready, Casanova."

Casanova turned smartly. Lorenzi stood before him, splendid in his nakedness like a young god. No trace of meanness lingered in his face. He seemed equally ready to kill or to die.

"What if I were to throw away my sword?" thought Casanova. "What if I were to embrace him?" He slipped the cloak from his shoulders and stood like Lorenzi, lean and naked.

Lorenzi lowered his point in salute, in accordance with the rules of fence. Casanova returned the salute. Next moment they crossed blades, and the steel glittered like silver in the sun.

"How long is it," thought Casanova, "since last I stood thus measuring sword with sword?" But none of his serious duels now recurred to his mind. He could think only of practice with the foils, such as ten years earlier he used to have every morning with his valet Costa, the rascal who afterwards bolted with a hundred and fifty thousand lire. "All the same, he was a fine fencer; nor has my hand forgotten its cunning! My arm is as true, my vision as keen, as ever..... Youth and age are fables. Am I not a god? Are we not both gods? If anyone could see us now. There are women who would pay a high price for the spectacle!"

The blades bent, the points sparkled; at each contact the rapiers sang softly in the morning air. "A fight? No, a fencing match! Why this look of horror, Marcolina? Are we not both worthy of your love? He is but a youngster; I am Casanova!"

Lorenzi sank to the ground, thrust through the heart. The sword fell from his grip. He opened his eyes wide, as if in utter astonishment. Once he raised his head for a moment, while his lips were fixed in a wry smile. Then the head fell back again, his nostrils dilated, there was a slight rattling in his throat, and he was dead.

Casanova bent over him, kneeled beside the body, saw a few drops of blood ooze from the wound, held his hand in front of Lorenzi's mouth—but the breath was stilled. A cold shiver passed through Casanova's frame. He rose and put on his cloak. Then, returning to the body, he glanced at the fallen youth, lying stark on the turf in incomparable beauty. The silence was broken by a soft rustling, as the morning breeze stirred the tree-tops.

"What shall I do?" Casanova asked himself. "Shall I summon aid? Olivo? Amalia? Marcolina? To what purpose? No one can bring him back to life."

He pondered with the calmness invariable to him in the most dangerous moments of his career. "It may be hours before anyone finds him; perhaps no one will come by before evening; perchance later still. That will give me time, and time is of the first importance."

He was still holding his sword. Noticing that it was bloody, he wiped it on the grass. He thought for a moment of dressing the corpse, but to do this would have involved the loss of precious and irrecoverable minutes. Paying the last duties, he bent once more and closed Lorenzi's eyes. "Lucky fellow," he murmured; and then, dreamily, he kissed the dead man's forehead.

He strode along beside the wall, turned the angle, and regained the road. The carriage was where he had left it, the coachman fast asleep on the box. Casanova was careful to avoid waking the man at first. Not until he had cautiously taken his seat did he call out: "Hullo, drive on, can't you?" and prodded him in the back. The startled coachman looked round, greatly astonished to find that it was broad daylight. Then he whipped up his horse and drove off.

Casanova sat far back in the carriage, wrapped in the cloak which had once belonged to Lorenzi. In the village a few children were to be seen in the streets, but it was plain that the elders were already at work in the fields. When the houses had been left behind Casanova drew a long breath. Opening the valise, he withdrew his clothes, and dressed beneath the cover of the cloak, somewhat concerned lest the coachman should turn and discover his fare's strange behavior. But nothing of the sort happened. Unmolested, Casanova was able to finish dressing, to pack away Lorenzi's cloak, and resume his own.

Glancing skyward, Casanova saw that the heavens were overcast. He had no sense of fatigue, but felt tense and wakeful. He thought over his situation, considering it from every possible point of view, and coming to the conclusion that, though grave, it was less alarming than it might have seemed to timid spirits. He would probably be suspected of having killed Lorenzi, but who could doubt that it had been in an honorable fight? Besides, Lorenzi had been lying in wait, had forced the encounter upon him, and no one could consider him a criminal for having fought in self-defence. But why had he left the body lying on the grass like that of a dead dog? Well, nobody could reproach him on that account. To flee away swiftly had been well within his right, had been almost a duty. In his place, Lorenzi would have done the same. But perhaps Venice would hand him over? Directly he arrived, he would claim the protection of his patron Bragadino. Yet this might involve his accusing himself of a deed which would after all remain undiscovered, or at any rate would perhaps never be laid to his charge. What proof was there against him? Had he not been summoned to Venice? Who could say that he went thither as a fugitive from justice? The coachman maybe, who had waited for him half the night. One or two additional gold pieces would stop the fellow's mouth.

Thus his thoughts ran in a circle. Suddenly he fancied he heard the sound of horses' hoofs from the road behind him. "Already?" was his first thought. He leaned over the side of the carriage to look backwards. All was clear. The carriage had driven past a farm, and the sound he had heard had been the echo of his own horse's hoofs. The discovery of this momentary self-deception quieted his apprehensions for a time, so that it seemed to him the danger was over. He could now see the towers of Mantua. "Drive on, man, drive on," he said under his breath, for he did not really wish the coachman to hear. The coachman, nearing the goal, had given the horse his head. Soon they reached the gate through which Casanova had left the town with Olivo less than forty-eight hours earlier. He told the coachman the name of the inn, and in a few minutes the carriage drew up at the sign of the Golden Lion.

# CHAPTER XI.

Casanova leaped from the carriage. The hostess stood in the doorway. She was bright and smiling, in the mood apparently to give Casanova the warm welcome of a lover whose absence has been regretted and whose return has been eagerly desired. But Casanova looked warningly towards the coachman, implying that the man might be an inconvenient witness, and then told him to eat and drink to his heart's content.

"A letter from Venice arrived for you yesterday, Chevalier," announced the hostess.

"Another?" enquired Casanova, going upstairs to his room.

The hostess followed. A sealed despatch was lying on the table. Casanova opened it in great excitement. He was anxious lest it should prove to be a revocation of the former offer. But the missive contained no more than a few lines from Bragadino, enclosing a draft for two hundred and fifty lire, in order that Casanova, should he have made up his mind to accept, might instantly set out for Venice.

Turning to the hostess, Casanova explained with an air of well-simulated vexation that he was unfortunately compelled to continue his journey instantly. Were he to delay, he would risk losing the post which his friend Bragadino had procured for him in Venice, a post for which there were fully a hundred applicants. Threatening clouds gathered on the hostess' face, so Casanova was prompt to add that all he proposed was to make sure of the appointment and to receive his patent as secretary to the Supreme Council. As soon as he was installed in office, he would ask permission to return to Mantua, that he might arrange his affairs. Of course this request could not be refused. He was going to leave most of his effects here. When he returned, it would only depend upon his beloved and charming friend whether she would give up inn-keeping and accompany him to Venice as his wife. She threw her arms round his neck, and with brimming eyes asked him whether before starting he would not at least make a good breakfast, if she might bring it up to his room. He knew she had in mind to provide a farewell feast, and though he felt no appetite for it, he agreed to the suggestion simply to be rid of her.

As soon as she was gone, he packed his bag with such underclothing and books as he urgently needed. Then, making his way to the parlor, where the coachman was enjoying a generous meal, he asked the man whether, for a sum which was more than double the usual fare, he would with the same horse drive along the Venice road as far as the next posting station. The coachman agreed without demur, thus relieving Casanova of his principal anxiety for the time.

Now the hostess entered, flushed with annoyance, to ask whether he had forgotten that his breakfast was awaiting him in his room. Casanova nonchalantly replied that he had not forgotten for a moment, and begged her, since he was short of time, to take his draft to the bank, and to bring back the two hundred and fifty lire. While she was hastening to fetch the money, Casanova returned to his room, and began to eat with wolfish voracity. He continued his meal when the hostess came back; stopping merely for an instant to pocket the money she brought him.

When he had finished eating, he turned to the woman. Thinking that her hour had at length come, she had drawn near, and was pressing up against him in a manner which could not be misunderstood. He clasped her somewhat roughly, kissed her on both cheeks, and, although she was obviously ready to grant him the last favors then and there, exclaimed: "I must be off. Till our next meeting!" He tore himself away with such violence that she fell back on to the corner of the couch. Her expression, with its mingling of disappointment, rage, and impotence, was so irresistibly funny that Casanova, as he closed the door behind him, burst out laughing.

The coachman could not fail to realize that his fare was in a hurry, but it was not his business to ask questions. He sat ready on the box when Casanova came out of the inn, and whipped up the horse the very moment the passenger was seated. On his own initiative he decided not to drive through the town, but to skirt it, and to rejoin the posting road upon the other side. The sun was not yet high, for it was only nine o'clock. Casanova reflected: "It is likely enough that Lorenzi's body has not been found yet." He hardly troubled to think that he himself had killed Lorenzi. All he knew was that he was glad to be leaving Mantua farther and farther behind, and glad to have rest at last.

He fell into a deep sleep, the deepest he had ever known. It lasted practically two days and two nights. The brief interruptions to his slumbers necessitated by the change of horses from time to time, and the interruptions that occurred when he was sitting in inns, or walking up and down in front of posting stations, or exchanging a few casual words with postmasters, innkeepers, customhouse officers, and travellers, did not linger in his memory as individual details. Thus it came to pass that the remembrance of these two days and nights merged as it were into the dream he had dreamed in Marcolina's bed. Even the duel between the two naked men upon the green turf in the early sunshine seemed somehow to belong to this dream, wherein often enough, in enigmatic fashion, he was not Casanova but Lorenzi; not the victor but the vanquished; not the fugitive, but the slain round whose pale young body the lonely wind of morning played. Neither he nor Lorenzi was any more real than were the senators in the purple robes who had knelt before him like beggars; nor any less real than such as that old fellow leaning against the parapet of a bridge, to whom at nightfall he had thrown alms from the carriage. Had not Casanova bent his powers of reason to the task of distinguishing between real experiences and dream experiences, he might well have imagined that in Marcolina's arms he had fallen into a mad dream from which he did not awaken until he caught sight of the Campanile of Venice.

# CHAPTER XII.

It was on the third morning of his journey that Casanova, having reached Mestre, sighted once more the bell tower after over twenty years of longing—a pillar of grey stone looming distantly in the twilight. It was but two leagues now to the beloved city in which he had been young. He paid the driver without remembering whether this was the fifth or the sixth with whom he had had to settle since quitting Mantua, and, followed by a lad carrying his baggage, walked through the mean streets to the harbor from which to-day, just as five-and-twenty years earlier, the boat was to leave for Venice at six in the morning.

The vessel seemed to have been waiting for him; hardly had he seated himself upon a narrow bench, among petty traders, manual workers, and women bringing their wares to market, when she cast off. It was a cloudy morning; mist was rolling across the lagoons; there was a smell of bilge-water, damp wood, fish, and fruit. The Campanile grew ever higher; additional towers appeared; cupolas became visible. The light of the morning sun was reflected from one roof, from two, from many. Individual houses were distinguishable, growing larger by degrees. Boats, great and small, showed through the mist; greetings were shouted from vessel to vessel. The chatter around him grew louder. A little girl offered him some grapes for sale. Munching the purple berries, he spat the skins over the side after the manner of his countrymen. He entered into friendly talk with someone who expressed satisfaction that the weather seemed to be clearing at last.

"What, has it been raining here for three days? That is news to me. I come from the south, from Naples and Rome."

The boat had entered the canals of the suburbs. Sordid houses stared at him with dirty windows, as if with vacant, hostile eyes. Twice or thrice the vessel stopped at a quay, and passengers came aboard; young fellows, one of whom had a great portfolio under his arm; women with baskets.

Here, at last, was familiar ground. Was not that the church where Martina used to go to confession? Was not that the house in which, after his own fashion, he had restored the pallid and dying Agatha to ruddy health? Was not that the place in which he had dealt with the charming Sylvia's rascal of a brother, had beaten the fellow black and blue? Up that canal to the right, in the small yellow house upon whose splashed steps the fat, bare-footed woman was standing....

Before he had fully recaptured the distant memory attaching to the house in question, the boat had entered the Grand Canal, and was passing slowly up the broad waterway with palaces on either hand. To Casanova, in his dreamy reflections, it seemed as if but yesterday he had traversed the same route.

He disembarked at the Rialto Bridge, for, before visiting Signor Bragadino, he wished to make sure of a room in a modest hostelry nearby—he knew where it was, though he could not recall the name. The place seemed more decayed, or at least more neglected, than he remembered it of old. A sulky waiter, badly in need of a shave, showed him to an uninviting room looking upon the blind wall of a house opposite. Casanova had no time to lose. Moreover, since he had spent nearly all his cash on the journey, the cheapness of these quarters was a great attraction. He decided, therefore, to make his lodging there for the present. Having removed the stains of travel, he deliberated for a while whether to put on his finer suit; then decided it was better to wear the soberer raiment, and walked out of the inn.

It was but a hundred paces, along a narrow alley and across a bridge, to Bragadino's small but elegant palace. A young servingman with a rather impudent manner took in Casanova's name in a way which implied that its celebrity had no meaning for him. Returning from his master's apartments with a more civil demeanor, he bade the guest enter.

Bragadino was seated at breakfast beside the open window, and made as if to rise; but Casanova begged him not to disturb himself.

"My dear Casanova," exclaimed Bragadino, "How delighted I am to see you once more! Who would have thought we should ever meet again?" He extended both hands to the newcomer.

Casanova seized them as if to kiss them, but did not do so. He answered the cordial greeting with warm words of thanks in the grandiloquent manner usual to him on such occasions. Bragadino begged him to be seated, and asked him whether he had breakfasted. Told that his guest was still fasting, Bragadino rang for his servant and gave the necessary orders. As soon as the man had gone, Bragadino expressed his gratification that Casanova had so unreservedly accepted the Supreme Council's offer. He would certainly not suffer for having decided to devote himself to the service of his country. Casanova responded by saying that he would deem himself happy if he could but win the Council's approval.

Such were Casanova's words, while his thoughts ran on. He could no longer detect in himself any feeling of hatred towards Bragadino. Nay, he realized that he was rather sorry for this man advanced in years and grown a trifle foolish, who sat facing him with a sparse white beard and red-rimmed eyes, and whose skinny hand trembled as he held his cup. The last time Casanova had seen him, Bragadino had probably been about as old as Casanova was to-day; but even then, to Casanova, Bragadino had seemed an old man.

The servant brought in Casanova's breakfast. The guest needed little pressing to induce him to make a hearty meal, for on the road he had had no more than a few snacks.

"I have journeyed here from Mantua without pausing for a night's rest, so eager was I to show my readiness to serve the Council and to prove my undying gratitude to my benefactor."—This was his excuse for the almost unmannerly greed with which he gulped down the steaming chocolate.

Through the window, from the Grand Canal and the lesser canals, rose the manifold noises of Venetian life. All other sounds were dominated by the monotonous shouts of the gondoliers. Somewhere close at hand, perhaps in the opposite palace (was it not the Fogazzari palace?), a woman with a fine soprano voice was practising; the singer was young—someone who could not have been born at the time when Casanova escaped from The Leads.

He ate rolls and butter, eggs, cold meat, continually excusing himself for his outrageous hunger, while Bragadino looked on well pleased.

"I do like young people to have a healthy appetite," said the Senator. "As far as I can remember, my dear Casanova, you have always been a good trencherman!" He recalled to mind a meal which he and Casanova had enjoyed together in the early days of their acquaintance. "Or rather, as now, I sat looking on while you ate. I had not taken a long walk, as you had. It was shortly after you had kicked that physician out of the house, the man who had almost been the death of me with his perpetual bleedings."

They went on talking of old times—when life had been better in Venice than it was to-day.

"Not everywhere," said Casanova, with a smiling allusion to The Leads.

Bragadino waved away the suggestion, as if this were not a suitable time for a reference to such petty disagreeables. "Besides, you must know that I did everything I could to save you from punishment, though unfortunately my efforts proved unavailing. Of course, if in those days I had already been a member of the Council of Ten!"

This broached the topic of political affairs. Warming to his theme, the old man recovered much of the wit and liveliness of earlier days. He told Casanova many remarkable details concerning the unfortunate tendencies which had recently begun to affect some of the Venetian youth, and concerning the dangerous intrigues of which infallible signs were now becoming manifest.

Casanova was thus well posted for his work. He spent the day in the gloomy chamber at the inn; and, simply as a means to secure calm after the recent excitements, he passed the hours in arranging his papers, and in burning those of which he wished to be rid. When evening fell, he made his way to the Café Quadri in the Square of St. Mark, since this was supposed to be the chief haunt of the freethinkers and revolutionists. Here he was promptly recognized by an elderly musician who had at one time been conductor of the orchestra in the San Samueli Theatre, where Casanova had been a violinist thirty years before. By this old acquaintance, and without any advances on his own part, he was introduced to the company. Most of them were young men, and many of their names were those which Bragadino had mentioned in the morning as belonging to persons of suspicious character.

But the name of Casanova did not produce upon his new acquaintances the effect which he felt himself entitled to anticipate. It was plain that most of them knew nothing more of Casanova than that, a great many years ago, he had for one reason or another, and perhaps for no reason at all, been imprisoned in The Leads;

and that, surmounting all possible dangers, he had made his escape. The booklet wherein, some years earlier, he had given so lively a description of his flight, had not indeed passed unnoticed; but no one seemed to have read it with sufficient attention. Casanova found it amusing to reflect that it lay within his power to help everyone of these young gentlemen to a speedy personal experience of the conditions of prison life in The Leads, and to a realization of the difficulties of escape. He was far, however, from betraying the slightest trace that he harbored so ill-natured an idea. On the contrary, he was able to play the innocent and to adopt an amiable rôle. After his usual fashion, he entertained the company by recounting all sorts of lively adventures, describing them as experiences he had had during his last journey from Rome to Venice. In substance these incidents were true enough, but they all dated from fifteen or twenty years earlier. He secured an eager and interested audience.

Another member of the company announced as a noteworthy item of news that an officer of Mantua on a visit to a friend, a neighboring landowner, had been murdered, and that the robbers had stripped him to the skin. The story attracted no particular attention, for in those days such occurrences were far from rare. Casanova resumed his narrative where it had been interrupted, resumed it as if this Mantua affair concerned him just as little as it concerned the rest of the company. In fact, being now freed from a disquiet whose existence he had hardly been willing to admit even to himself, his manner became brighter and bolder than ever.

It was past midnight when, after a light-hearted farewell, he walked alone across the wide, empty square. The heavens were veiled in luminous mist. He moved with the confident step of a sleep-walker. Without being really conscious that he was on a path which he had not traversed for five-and-twenty years, he found the way through tortuous alleys, between dark houses, and over narrow bridges. At length he reached the dilapidated inn, and had to knock repeatedly before the door was opened to him with a slow unfriendliness.

When, a few minutes later, having but half undressed, he threw himself upon his uneasy pallet, he was overwhelmed with a weariness amounting to pain, while upon his lips was a bitter after-taste which seemed to permeate his whole being. Thus, at the close of his long exile, did he first woo sleep in the city to which he had so eagerly desired to return. And here, when morning was about to break, the heavy and dreamless sleep of exhaustion came to console the aging adventurer.

**THE END.**

# POSTFACE

It is a historical fact that Casanova visited Voltaire at Ferney. There is, however, no historical warrant for the account of the matter given in the foregoing novel, and still less for the statement that Casanova wrote a polemic against Voltaire. It is a historical fact, likewise, that Casanova, when between fifty and sixty years of age, found it necessary to enter Venetian service as a spy. Of this, and of many other doings of the celebrated adventurer to which casual allusion is made in the course of the novel, fuller and more accurate accounts will be found in Casanova's *Memoirs*. Speaking generally, nevertheless, *Casanova's Homecoming* is to be regarded throughout as a work of fiction.

A. S.

Lector House believes that a society develops through a two-fold approach of continuous learning and adaptation, which is derived from the study of classic literary works spread across the historic timeline of literature records. Therefore, we aim at reviving, repairing and redeveloping all those inaccessible or damaged but historically as well as culturally important literature across subjects so that the future generations may have an opportunity to study and learn from past works to embark upon a journey of creating a better future.

This book is a result of an effort made by Lector House towards making a contribution to the preservation and repair of original ancient works which might hold historical significance to the approach of continuous learning across subjects.

HAPPY READING & LEARNING!

LECTOR HOUSE

LECTOR HOUSE LLP
E-MAIL: info@lectorhouse.com

9 789356 146426

9 789356 146426

Printed by Libri Plureos GmbH in Hamburg,
Germany